# Starting Over

Robyn C Rye

Published by robyncrye, 2023.

# Also by Robyn C Rye

**Farnsworth Sisters**
Marrying a Rogue
Rescuing Hannah

**The Buckingham Sisters**
Lady Maggie's Challenge
Layla's Unwanted Husband

**The Evans Family**
Sometimes Love is not Enough
Still the One
Moving Forward

**Standalone**
One More Chance
Lady Jayne's Reputation
Third Time's the Charm
Can't Stop Loving You

The Marriage Scam
An Unlikely Match
Searching For You
The Unexpected Suitor
The Lady and the Duke
Starting Over
An Unforgettable Stranger
The Duke's Revenge
The Temporary Wife
Against The Odds
Betrayed
No Good Turn Goes Unpunished
Lady Eloise's Soldier
Lillian's Forbidden Beau
Remember Me
Always Second Best
When One Door Closes
Coming Home to You
Chasing Shadows
Fool Me Once
Deserting Lady Audrey
My Unlikely Saviour
Lies and Deception
A New Beginning
Julia's Second Chance
The Hidden Enemy
The Maiden's Redemption
Miss Elizabeth's Season

# Table of Contents

# Author's Note

As a reader, you may wonder why some words seem misspelt, but as an Australian writer, I use English spellings rather than American ones. I have used the spell check, but with an Australian slant.

I loved recounting the story of Brett and Jacqui, and I hope you enjoyed the unfolding tale of their trials and successes.

If you enjoyed the book and have a moment, I would appreciate a brief review on the page or site where you purchased it. Your help in spreading the word is appreciated. Reviews from readers like you make a massive difference in helping new readers find stories like ***Starting Over.***

**Contact me at**
*robyncrye.author@gmail.com*

# Chapter One

B*rett*

The ambulance drew away from the house with lights flashing. Brett raced for his ute. The paramedics refused to allow him to travel in their vehicle, so there was no alternative but to follow. The ute rattled over the grid, and Brett jammed the accelerator hard, following in the wake of the emergency vehicle.

He had returned home earlier to discover the unconscious figure of his mum on the kitchen floor. During the morning, while feeding stock, he hadn't thought to check her, even though she was unwell when he left. Who would suspect a minor ailment would cause a dash to the hospital? Guilt and shame overwhelmed him. Why hadn't he checked to see how she felt?

Hurtling along the unmade road toward Lonsdale was a nightmare. An unusual noise drew Brett's attention to the ambulance; the wail of the siren chilled his blood. Hopefully, the siren made a path for the vehicle and was not a sign of his mother's deteriorating condition.

The traffic lights were red as the two vehicles reached the central junction. The driver hit the horn, wailing a warning to others who were ready to enter the crossroad. Brett cursed the lights, which remained red, preventing him from following the ambulance. Stuck at the lights as the ambulance disappeared into the distance, Brett muttered obscenities while waiting for the other vehicles to clear the intersection.

Upon reaching the hospital, he discovered that the lights and sirens had ceased, and the ambulance was pulling into the emergency bay. Attendants rushed to meet the gurney. Medics ran alongside, attempting to keep pace with the fast-moving stretcher, assessing and treating as the gurney disappeared into the building.

Brett watched the procession with dread. The medical staff was grim-faced and severe, and there was no way of knowing how critical the illness was. The door to the room that the gurney and attendants entered slammed shut, shutting him out.

A woman with a kind smile stood behind the service counter.

"Are you the next of kin?"

"Yes, and I need to be with her," he said.

"Sorry, but the doctors need to treat patients without the distraction of friends and relatives. They're doing their best, and you can do nothing to help. Come and fill in the admission forms," she said.

"When will someone tell me what is wrong?"

"I'm not sure. Why don't we handle the admission paperwork, and then you can go to the waiting room? If you want to clean up, a bathroom is off to the side."

Brett filled out the forms, which took a while. He retreated to the waiting room and followed the nurse's suggestion to wash quickly. As he caught sight of his reflection in the mirror, he cringed at the grime from the paddock that covered his face, hands, and forearms.

After cleaning up, Brett paced backwards and forwards. People watched his actions with curiosity. Dirt and dust coated his clothes, but not offending others was a low priority. Damn! This tragedy was his fault. If he hadn't been in such a rush to leave this morning, he might have realised that his mum was critically ill and taken her to the hospital. Earlier medical intervention may have yielded a different outcome. What felt like aeons later, a doctor walked back into the waiting room, his expression grim.

"Mr Sanderson, I'm Doctor Madden. Before transporting your mother to the hospital, I suspect she suffered a mild heart attack. The paramedics revived her, but she had another cardiac arrest on arrival at the hospital. I'm sorry, Mr Sanderson. We did all we could, but couldn't save your mother."

The sudden pain in Brett's stomach doubled him over. With the help of a nurse, she guided him to the bank of seats and eased him into a chair. Dizziness assailed him, and his stomach began doing somersaults. The nurse provided a sick bag when the greenish tinge on his face became noticeable. He heaved and reached. When the sickness passed, he sat, head in his hands, chin quivering as his eyes prickled with tears. The nurse brought a drink, and the cold water soothed his aching throat but did nothing to dislodge the boulder in his chest. He had to complete a different type of paperwork now that his mother had no hope.

Brett said, "I can't do this now."

The nurse nodded and patted his shoulder.

"The rest of the paperwork can wait until later. I have the most important information. Is there someone you want me to call? A relative or friend, perhaps?"

He gave a grim laugh. "No, there's no one."

# Chapter Two

*J*acqui

Jacqui sat at her desk with a stack of test papers in front of her. It was practically four o'clock, a few more minutes, and she hoped to finish marking the last article. When the phone rang, Jacqui groaned. A chatty colleague was the last thing she needed.

"Hello, Jacqui speaking."

"Jacqui, it's Don. Can you come past here as you leave? I need a quick word."

"Don, can it wait until tomorrow? I want to finish marking the tests."

"Okay, but call past tomorrow morning, first thing."

When she arrived home, the flag on the mailbox was up, showing there was mail. After collecting the delivery, she sorted the letters as she walked towards the front door. Postmarked in Brisbane that morning, one envelope from the education department stood out from the others. Curious about the contents, she ripped open the envelope. Eyes wide in disbelief, an anguished cry escaped her mouth. Her legs buckled, and she sank into the nearest chair. How could this be happening?

With year seven students moving to high schools, everyone wondered where the extra staff from primary schools might find placements. The government informed the teachers that the relocation of excess staff was imminent and that everyone at the school had to select their preferred option. The options were either to transfer to a secondary school or to move to a new school. As with most of the other teachers, Jacqui had thought that this change wouldn't affect her. How wrong she had been!

In a moment of clarity, Jacqui realised the boss had intended to inform her that she should expect the letter, but the department had acted more quickly. Could the union help? The question was moot. She looked at the clock and realised that the union advisors had finished for the day. Advice could wait until tomorrow.

A country posting filled her with dread. Not that she didn't appreciate the country. The country was beautiful. However, she would have applied for a country posting if she wanted to live there.

That night, Jacqui tossed and turned in bed, unable to sleep. Scalding tears filled her eyes. Departing from the school meant leaving the kids in her class and leaving home. The government's high-handed action in transferring unwilling teachers to other schools was unfair. This decision would completely disrupt her life. She had to pack up and leave four weeks before the mid-break holidays. Where the hell was Manwarring?

Her meeting the following day was brief. The boss noticed her red eyes and grim expression.

"I see you've received the news. I'll be sorry to lose you, but as one of the few staff members who haven't done country service, you're limited in your options. What will you do?"

"Contact the union?" Jacqui queried.

"You're welcome to do that, but they won't be able to help. It will be challenging to argue a case for staying here without a spouse or children to use as leverage. As far as the department is concerned, you're unencumbered. Regardless of your choice, it comes into play on the first day of the next term. Don't dally around too long; you'll need time to adjust to your transfer."

What was her mother going to say when told of the transfer? She knew her mother considered her teaching job a hobby. According to her mother, Jacqui's role in life was to meet a professional man, get married, and have an acceptable number of grandchildren. No matter how many dates she had turned down, her mother still saw Jacqui as a child who needed guidance. Her mother's advice was always towards activities and people who verified her social standing in the neighbourhood; she admitted that her mother was a snob.

Jacqui raced into the house. This morning, she selected the clothes for the night and laid them on the bed. She grimaced as she viewed the clothes put aside for tonight's dinner. The tailored skirt and the demure blouse were her mother's ideas of what a lady wore. When her mother heard the news of the posting to the country, she would be furious; why not dress in comfortable clothes? What the hell, she muttered. Balling up the clothes from the bed, she launched them at the wastepaper bin, mindful that she was the one to clean up after herself later.

A quick rummage through her closet produced a pair of white jeans and a blue halter-necked top. Jacqui pulled on the snug-fitting jeans, aware that they showed off her long legs. Breathing in, she snapped the button at the waistband. Although the jeans hugged her generous hips and bottom, they looked dressy enough to evade her mother's disdain. The blue halter neck exposed smooth white shoulders and enough cleavage to make her feel daring. Flat-heeled sandals and dangling earrings completed the ensemble. Jacqui ran a brush through her wavy, brown hair and felt the stylish short style swing loosely around her face. She grabbed her bag and raced for the door.

She smiled as she walked along the driveway towards her car. The sight of her new vehicle never grew old. Recently, she traded her old clunker for a sporty, red model. Her father helped her choose it, and Jacqui purchased the car she wanted despite her mother's warnings that she should buy a family sedan.

As she guided her vehicle along the road, the landmarks she passed indicated that this was home. She had grown up in this suburb and stayed when her parents sold their modest home to move to the most private part of the new estate at Kyogle. She couldn't see sense in leaving familiar surroundings and friendly neighbours, but then she thought her mother had never fit in.

# STARTING OVER

The forty-minute trip from her place to her parents' home in Kyogle always intrigued her. The area looked like the town planners had come in and designated spots for different dwellings.

Jacqui arrived at her parents' home later than she had expected. She had been parking on the street until recently, but her neighbour's opinions worried her mother. As she navigated the long driveway, she barely drew breath. The entrance meandered through manicured lawns and beautiful gardens, and the thought of straying from the narrow path and leaving a mark on the grass made her break out in a sweat.

"Mum, where are you?"

"Jacqui, must you shout like a fishwife? I am in the kitchen if you are coming for dinner." She eyed her daughter's clothes with apparent distaste. Her eyebrows raised and her mouth pursed, her gaze strayed from Jacqui's flat heels to the dangly earrings.

"You said you had news to share. You can tell me now, and we can catch your father up later," said Margaret Stuart.

"Um, if you don't mind, I'll wait until dinner, and then I can tell you both together."

Her mother sniffed to show her displeasure.

They ate dinner in the formal dining room. The room was chilly, and the furnishings were dark, antique pieces. Jacqui's brother, Patrick, called this place the morgue, but never in his mother's hearing. The meal was exquisite, as always. Her mother tried to impress when entertaining, even though it was only Jacqui tonight.

"Ok, Jac. Tell us your news," said Colin Stuart, her dad.

"This is disturbing, I know, but I'd appreciate it if you could refrain from commenting until I finish." She raised her eyebrow in question at her mother, who nodded.

"There is an oversupply of primary teachers because of the changes to the school system. Secondary schools need additional teachers to cover the extra classes. Primary teachers could nominate to change over to high schools, and if they didn't want to, the education department would decide what to do with the surplus staff."

"Well, that sounds reasonable," said her father.

Jacqui nodded. "The problem is, what should we do with the excess staff? Therefore, the department will relocate the staff who haven't completed their country service to the country in question. That's me. I'm to transfer to a country town called Manwarring."

Jacqui's mother let out a gasp of disbelief.

"Colin, you must use your contacts to change this! I can't bear the thought of our daughter in some rural backwater."

"Sorry, Margaret, but I know no one in the education department, and I'm not sure that rattling cages won't make this worse. What's the length of the posting in a country school, Jac?"

"A transfer is around three years. The problem, though, is once you're there, the department forgets you exist unless you keep on their case."

"Well, that sorts it," said Margaret Stuart. "It's time you forgot this teaching foolishness and settled down. You can join committees, and I can introduce you to young men. Ring the education department on Monday and quit."

"Sorry, Mum, that will not happen. I don't want to play ladies and join your committees, and I don't want introductions to pompous, self-opinionated men who consider themselves God's gift. When I find a man, he will be unpretentious and genuine, and his bank account won't come into it," said Jacqui.

"Colin, speak to your daughter! How can we allow this to happen? Jacqui, you won't meet any reasonable men out there. When you return home from the country posting, you will be too old for young professional men to take a chance on," said Margaret.

"Margaret, you're overlooking a small detail; Jacqui doesn't want a man at this stage, and she doesn't want to quit. Am I right, Jac?" her father asked.

"Yes! I can't understand your old-fashioned ideas, Mum. I won't be too old at thirty or even thirty-five to marry; I'm only twenty-seven now. You sound like the dowagers in the olden days, when they organised suitable marriages for eighteen-year-old girls. We are in the twenty-first century, not the nineteenth. I intend to teach and will get a posting back as soon as possible."

"When do you need to be there, Jac?" her father asked.

"At the start of the new term. I'll take long service leave for the next two weeks, allowing me to wrap up everything here. If I pack clothes and resources, I hope to find a place to rent quickly. Manwarring has accommodation at the pub; that will do for a start while I find something more suitable."

Margaret looked ill at the thought of her daughter living at a pub. A spark of an idea formed; by introducing her daughter to enough eligible men in the next two weeks, she might convince Jacqui to change her plans.

"Well, it appears I don't get to voice my opinion. Why don't you move here for the next two weeks, which will allow you to vacate your flat?" said Margaret.

Over the next two weeks, Margaret subjected Jacqui to many dinner companions. She couldn't believe her mother had outsmarted her. Her mother decreed that she dress up for meals, style her hair and wear makeup, something Jacqui rarely did. The eligible men were all cut from the same template. They dressed immaculately, and most sported suits with designer labels. Despite having impeccable manners, most candidates had an air of self-importance. They showed no interest whatsoever in anything other than the financial market. In Jacqui's way of thinking, a character flaw is that none of the men have a sense of humour.

Jacqui was more than ready to vacate her parents' house and move to the country by the end of the two weeks.

# Chapter Three

B *rett*

As the pallbearers lowered the coffin, a wave of grief engulfed Brett. The sensation was so intense that he feared he might keel over. For the last thirty-two years, his mother had been the one constant in his life. After his father's death, he believed she was his only family. As an only child, he barely missed the company of siblings; his parents provided the support and comfort he needed.

With his father's death and the death of his grandparents years earlier, he and his mother became even closer. She was his mother, business partner and friend. The well-meaning mourners, with their offers of "Call me if you need anything", would fade away, leaving him alone.

In the company of his newly discovered Aunt Gloria, the younger sister of his father, Brett, entered the church hall. Brett didn't understand how this woman had heard about his mother's death or even from where she had come. She turned up at the farm, announced that she was his aunt and pitched in to help him organise the funeral. The church ladies offered to provide light refreshments, and he gratefully accepted. He could hear the clinking of cups on saucers and the muted tone of the people as they partook of the food. While he wasn't up to socialising, he knew people expected him to walk around so they could offer their condolences.

Aunt Gloria came and bullied him into having a cup of tea, and when the other mourners took their leave, she ushered him outside to his battered old ute. On the drive home, he found himself accompanied by a woman he didn't know. Once they arrived, she set herself up in one of the spare bedrooms and urged him to get on with his jobs; she would organise dinner. Bemused by the turn of events, Brett walked outside to begin the evening's tasks.

In bed that night, unable to sleep, thoughts of the decisions he needed to make ran through his mind. He and his mother never talked about the future. Who would imagine that she would become ill and leave him alone? Would she want him to sell now that he was by himself? They should have made that decision a long time ago. No matter how hard he tried, he couldn't see his mother in a retirement village. Life on the land was hard, but she never wanted to leave. Would selling the farm now be a betrayal of her trust? The property and anything else she owned were now his, but did he have the right to give up the life she had given him?

His thoughts returned to the present and the farm's operation. He was unlikely to be able to work the farm single-handedly, so he needed to employ a farmhand. The problem with hiring a worker was that he couldn't afford to pay someone. His mother always did the accounts, so this was another problem that he needed to solve. There never seemed to be enough time to complete the bookwork with the jobs outside. The futility of trying to keep the farm running overwhelmed him. Would there be any point in his struggling for a few more months or years? Lack of rain and a shortage of funds would be ongoing problems, ones he had no energy to deal with anymore.

Not sure what to do, Brett continued the routine jobs each day—the days rolled on, the same old tasks every day in the relentless heat. Brett felt like he was beating his head against a brick wall. Some mornings, he struggled to get out of bed. It would be much easier to pull the sheet back up and pretend that the day hadn't started. If it rained, there would be some green grass for the cattle, but apparently, that was asking too much. He fed them with religious regularity, praying for a break in the weather.

As the days moved into weeks, he realised his aunt intended to stay where she was. He was unsure how happy he was about her continued presence. Her company had advantages; she took care of the housekeeping and provided him with meals, but they hadn't discussed her tenancy. She seemed to think he needed a replacement mum, and while that was all right for a while, it didn't strike him as a lifetime plan. What was in it for her? He wondered. Didn't she have a life of her own? It was time to talk about her expected length of tenancy, but apathy gripped him. Anything more mundane than his daily jobs defeated him.

His aunt's constant queries about the farm's future forced him to admit that he hadn't gotten that far. Aunt Gloria thought his only choice would be to sell. There was merit in that thought, but the problem was that so much of his history was here, and it was a hard decision. Did he want to sell? What would he do, and where would he go if he could find a buyer? He had lived here all his life; was there something better in the city for him?

With his aunt out shopping, he sat in his office to do a 'for' and 'against' list regarding selling. His Mum believed in writing down all the benefits and problems associated with a decision, then weighing them up. His Aunt's persistence in raising the sale made him realise he needed to make a choice. He couldn't hang on indefinitely without coming to some resolution.

It had been a while since he sat behind the desk, but he knew the seat was not in its usual position this time. Someone had moved the chair to accommodate their shorter legs. It appeared his aunt had used the computer, and while that wasn't a problem, he would have preferred she check with him first. Frowning, he clicked on the laptop and waited for it to fire up. Brett searched, examining the computer's internet history. There were numerous hits on an agricultural real estate site. With growing unease, he took down the phone number of one business, intending to make some calls later.

What else was she doing if his aunt searched for real estate agents online? Brett accessed her e-mails to see if she had made any appointments with agents. Qualms about invading her privacy disappeared when he realised it was his farm she was dealing with. If he had asked her to do some research, that would be okay, but he hadn't. Her research was purely for herself.

To make matters worse, she used his office without asking him. He wondered what else she had accessed in the room. She had plenty of time to delve into his private files with him outside during the day.

Brett took a while to discover her password; after trying the property name, her surname, and a few other options, he finally hit upon her father's name. The e-mails were very revealing. His aunt was conspiring with someone else, and they intended to sell the property from under him and take off with the proceeds. What should he do? Confronting her without proof would allow her to wriggle out of his accusations with excuses of a misunderstanding. The need for evidence necessitated printing copies of the emails, checking the sent box, and copying the relevant emails.

With dread, he went to the filing cabinet to look for the deeds to the property. They were missing. Where would his aunt hide the title documents? He needed to know if there was time to search the house for the concealed documents. Brett wondered whether his aunt was on her way home yet. He tapped his fingers on the counter while listening to the phone ring. If Aunt Gloria didn't answer, she was on her way back. Just as he was about to give up, she answered the phone.

"Aunt Gloria, are you ready to come home yet?" Brett asked.

"Not yet. It might be a while before I finish the jobs in town. Did you want something?" Aunt Gloria said.

"No, I need to talk to you about something, but it will keep. I guess I'll see you in a while," Brett said.

Now, he knew there was enough time to search for the deeds; it would take his aunt more than an hour to drive home, and as she wasn't ready to leave yet, he had plenty of time. Brett searched methodically through his office and then worked through his aunt's room, after hunting through the drawers, cupboards and even under the mattress. Brett's stomach lurched. Where were the deeds? Desperate, he emptied a suitcase that still contained clothes, and there he found the documents hidden at the bottom in an envelope. He heaved a sigh of relief. He was grateful she hadn't taken the addressed letter with her that day.

He called the principal of the real estate agent. Because of the man's information, he took his problem to the local police and his solicitor. The two men arrived at the property within minutes of each other. Brett relayed the details of his discovery. Another phone call revealed that someone had notified the title's office of the need to change the document's details. The hold-up was that a copy of his mother's death certificate and the original deeds were necessary to alter the facts.

"Looks like you and I should complete the formalities so that this place is entirely yours," the solicitor said. "Come in tomorrow and fill out the paperwork."

The sound of a vehicle approaching heralded Aunt Gloria's arrival. Unaware of the trouble that awaited her, she called out, "Help me with the shopping, Brett."

He walked out to the car and grabbed a box of supplies while his aunt carried many bags. As she entered the kitchen, Aunt Gloria stopped short. Her eyebrows shot up, and her mouth gaped open.

"Hello, constable, to what do we owe the pleasure?"

Brett moved the shopping bags his aunt deposited on the table and placed the paperwork down. He showed her the emails, the letter with the title deeds, the phone number and name of the real estate office, and the claims office.

"Why did you have the deeds to my property in an addressed envelope? You have also been talking to an estate agent. Why, Aunt?" Brett asked.

Aunt Gloria's face paled, looking anxiously at Brett and the constable.

"Okay, ma'am, it would appear from our inquiries that you were all set to sell Brett's property. I am correct, aren't I?" the police officer,

Trent, asked. Aunt Gloria swallowed, and her face flushed. Her jaw tightened, and her lips compressed, forming a straight line.

"My brother intended to leave me half of the property; that bitch of a wife talked him out of it. It should be half my property. I need the money; I can't spend my whole life living in this backwater being a maid for Brett. He can't run this farm by himself. If it weren't for me, there wouldn't have been anyone to look after him over the last few months. If I sold the property, I thought we could share the money and start again elsewhere."

"Why is it right to decide without consulting me?" Brett asked.

"As for giving me the proceeds, that's bunkum; your friend Mr Rowan Wallace, to whom you were sending the deeds to falsify, says you intended to pay him for doctoring the deeds."

Aunt Gloria gasped at that news.

"Just one thing before you leave. Are you actually my aunt?" Brett asked.

"Yes, I am. I'm your only living relative, you ungrateful scum. After everything I've done for you over the last months, you intend to evict me? So much for family ties," she said.

Trent patted his arm. "What do they say? You can pick your friends, but you can't choose your family. I'll process this, and you'll need to come in and provide a formal statement. Catch up with me tomorrow, and I can tell you what will happen. In the meantime, think about whether you want to press charges. She is, after all, your aunt."

When the others left, Brett slumped down at the table. What was that saying? If it looks too good to be true, it probably is. How was he to know his aunt wanted the property? He took her at face value, assuming she was there to help. What a lack of judgment, he thought. I won't get caught again.

# Chapter Four

J*acqui*

When the time for Jacqui's departure arrived, a cocktail of emotions assailed her. There was sadness at leaving, but relief that there was no longer any need to converse politely with random men at dinner time. A niggle of excitement tugged at her mind. Her brother had left home years ago, and now the posting allowed Jacqui to make her own decisions, rather than being bullied into submission by her mother. This new posting could prove to be a godsend. Viewing the move as temporary, she was confident that she would survive the stint in the country.

Jacqui left Kyogle early, but with little previous country driving experience, she was sure regular breaks would be necessary. Even with rest breaks, her estimated arrival time in Manwarring was around four o'clock. The shops would still be open, and she could collect the school keys from the post office manager. There would be plenty of time to settle in at the pub before dinner.

The scenery on the city's outskirts changed from residential areas to industrial businesses and large warehouses. Vast tracts of undeveloped land on the outskirts were uninhabited, but occasionally, a shelter for horses was visible. The animals stood under the shade, heads drooping in the morning sun. A random horse snuffled in the barren dirt, looking for grass.

The further she drove, the less evidence of development she found. She realised that these vast spaces were farmers' paddocks. There were no signs of life, so the farmers must have built their residences far from the road. Is this how Manwarring would look? The vast wastelands bordering the road caused a niggle of concern. Could she live in a place that seemed all but uninhabited?

# STARTING OVER

The trip took longer than Jacqui expected. She needed to stop for petrol and coffee. The petrol stations were new, ultra-modern places in the city, but the country stations were old, shabby and manned by disinterested adolescents.

As the afternoon dragged on, it seemed to Jacqui that she had been driving forever. There was nothing to see out here except endless straight roads, barren ground and hollow-ribbed cattle. The dust followed her car like a persistent hitchhiker. A while ago, the place she passed through had enough inhabitants barely to call a town, just a pub, a corner store, and the rail depot. Her GPS showed she was due to arrive in another settlement soon, and the road to Manwarring branched off there.

A slow smile grew as she realised that the township of Lonsdale was a thriving country community. There was a shopping centre that boasted twelve specialty stores and a supermarket. After following the signs to Manwarring, Jacqui turned off the highway and discovered a single bitumen strip that continued as far as the eye could see. The endless stretch of the road sent shivers down her spine. Why hadn't she taken her dad's advice and traded in the sporty little Toyota for something better suited to the terrain? The trusty GPS showed that the distance to Manwarring was forty kilometres.

Shortly after this comforting thought, the single bitumen road dwindled into a dirt road full of potholes and strewn with roadkill. Large cattle trucks loaded with wide-eyed beasts with protruding ribs thundered past on the dirt road and forced her vehicle off the road. Jacqui gripped the steering wheel with a white-knuckled grip.

An hour later, she drove into Manwarring. The urge to burst into tears was overwhelming. After the harrowing trip, a pain throbbed at her temples, and her fingers ached from their tight grip on the steering wheel. She looked around. The township comprised a single main street. The pub, a corner shop, a café, the feed merchant's depot, a chemist, and the post office agency were on the main road. Her stomach lurched, and her shoulders sagged. By arriving so late, the businesses were all shut down for the night.

# Chapter Five

B*rett*

The skies darkened as though nightfall had arrived early. The sound of the wind whistled through the gum trees that surrounded the old homestead. Brett sprinted from the machinery shed to the veranda. He scanned the horizon, searching for the telltale plume of smoke that showed the location of the fire. There wasn't a plume of smoke; instead of flames, a cloud of dust roared toward the house. He raced through the house, closing windows and doors to minimise the mess that the dust storm would make.

The choking cloud of dust enveloped the entire property, blocking the sun, and Brett stood in pitch darkness, waiting for the storm to pass. After the dust had receded, an eerie quiet did little to settle his mood. Storms like this one originate from out west. Television news reports showed dust storms, but it was hard to imagine until you saw another bloke's topsoil blowing your way.

"God, this life is just the pits. Farming is for mugs. Every day is a never-ending battle against Mother Nature; first, we have a drought, and then there will be a flood," Brett grumbled. He knew the topsoil that the wind hadn't swept away in the drought would wash away in the next flood.

He looked around at the bare ground that was supposed to be pasture. He considered taking the stock out onto the stock routes, but there was probably no feed there. Other desperate farmers would have already grazed the stock routes out by now. Here, at least, his bores were holding up, so that was a blessing. Each day, he carted food to keep the hungry stock alive.

Farming alone contained a few benefits. There was no need to compromise your standards, but it was bloody lonely. Not to mention that when Brett finished outside, things inside needed doing; most notable was cooking a meal. When Aunt Gloria lived on the farm, she prepared meals and took care of the household chores. However, when someone intends to steal from you, all the hot meals in the universe couldn't convince you to extend their stay.

As he stood on the veranda, Brett thought of everything that needed to be done. The morning jobs, including hauling hay and cottonseed to the stock and pouring out litres of molasses to keep the cattle going, were done. The task was endless, but at least the stock was always happy to see him. The loose fence in the far paddock was on his to-do list. If he didn't fix it soon, whiney old Pratt would be on the phone complaining about wandering stock. Brett thought there was nothing to complain about; there was no grass in either of their paddocks, so that the cattle couldn't damage his pasture.

Should he forget the outside jobs today and do the housework instead? His mum would turn in her grave if she saw the house now. Her lovingly tended gardens were a wasteland of weeds. Brett could spare neither the time nor the water to keep up the plot. Perhaps he should collect the slasher and run it over the entire yard; it would be aeons before he had the time or energy to refurbish it. He scanned the exterior of the house. It needed a coat of paint, and a rail on the veranda required fixing. The jobs were never-ending, and of late, he had lost heart. The inside of the house wasn't much better. Before the dust storm blew through the house, a thin coat of dust covered much of the furniture, and the floors were no better. When was the last time he had changed the sheets on the bed?

He needed a maid to do the housework. Huh, how could he pay a housemaid? Money was tighter than water. A wife in the house, doing the inside jobs, was just a dream. None of the local girls wanted to marry a poor farmer. To interest the local girls, a bloke needed buckets of money and a flash car before the women gave you the time of day. He chuckled. Should he enter the TV show 'Farmer Wants a Wife'? He knew he looked okay, but doubted he had the finances or a house to interest the producers of such a show. Perhaps there could be a sequel called 'The Poor Farmer Wants a Wife'?

Brett watched the sun go behind a cloud, a cloud that promised much but was unlikely to deliver. He kicked his boots off at the back door and entered the kitchen. A quick appraisal of the kitchen had him gritting his teeth. Modern appliances looked out of place alongside the old wood stove and refrigerator. He hadn't lit the stove in months, but the hot plates had burned around the rings where his cookery attempts failed. The benches were wood-grained under the profusion of dishes and half-eaten sandwiches, and the cupboards were a pale yellow.

He would have a slap-up dinner and then tackle the housework. The problem with the slap-up meal was that the freezer and cupboards were empty. When had he been shopping last? He would go to the pub for dinner and shop the next day. The bar in Manwarring wasn't much. It was a dump, but there was no other place in town to get a feed after hours. A meal and two or three beers might put a more positive spin on his life.

# Chapter Six

After parking outside the pub, the only business still open, Jacqui stretched and walked towards the door. The building's exterior needed repair; she hoped the interior was in better condition. She eyed the unpainted weatherboards and the moss-covered bluestone as she walked across the warped veranda.

The interior of the building was dimly lit, and the furnishings were worn and shabby. Wooden panelling lined the walls, and the low lighting obscured the drinkers. Heavy wooden tables and bench seats inhabited the open spaces, and a long wooden bar dominated the room. Cigarette smoke swirled in the air, and the smell of stale beer and body odour wafted off the patron's clothes. The unpleasant odours in the room assaulted her senses, and she wondered at the wisdom of seeking accommodation here.

"What do you want, missy?" boomed a man's voice.

"Ah, hi. I'm a new schoolteacher. I'm looking for a room to rent."

"No lodgings here, luv."

"Is the publican on the premises? Can I talk to him?"

"I'm the landlord, and there are no rooms to rent."

"Well, where does the other teacher live? He might let me bunk in with him until something else becomes available."

The publican laughed and winked at the men sitting at the bar. "There is no other teacher. As soon as the department announced your appointment, he cleared out."

Jacqui sucked in a quick breath. If a male teacher couldn't handle these Neanderthals, what chance did she have?

"Where did he live?"

"He stayed here, but I don't think you can stay here. Sheila causes nothing but problems at a pub."

Jacqui gritted her teeth. "I need accommodation. What if I come in through the back door, rather than through the bar? That shouldn't inconvenience you?"

"I said no, and I mean no."

Her hands shook, and her lips trembled, but she would not cry in front of these degenerates.

"You can stay with me," said a drunken middle-aged man. He leered at her. "I'm sure we can come to an arrangement."

The drinkers laughed, and others made accommodation offers with the same insinuations. Jacqui sighed and closed her eyes.

"Are there any married blokes here?"

"Yeah, I'm married, and my missus would skin me alive if I arrived home with you," said a man seated at the bar.

Jacqui's gaze flittered over the occupants of the bar. At the far end, a man sat alone, his hat on the bar and his back hunched over a pot of beer. He averted his face, distancing himself from the conversation. Well, no help there, thought Jacqui.

Disheartened, she walked out to the car. What a great welcome to the country! What happened to the famed country people's friendliness? Driving back along the dirt road at night made her cringe. Sleeping in the car was not an option since she had loaded the boot and back seat with luggage. Even using the school building to sleep in tonight was out of the question because the keys were in the post office.

A fresh breeze blew through the car's open window. She shivered. With a chilly night coming up, there was no choice but to turn around and drive back to Lonsdale. A man emerged from the pub; it was the bloke who had sat at the end of the bar. He was tall and well-built, his athletic body tanned and well-defined. A shock of brown hair that needed a cut, along with brown stubble, added a rakish air. He wore what city folk assumed was the mandatory dress for countrymen: blue jeans, a shirt, and boots.

"Hi, I'm Brett Sanderson. I can help if you're okay with being teased for accepting my offer."

"Hello, I'm Jacqui Stuart. If the proposal is another lewd suggestion, then forget it."

Jacqui watched as he twisted his hat in his hands. After taking a big breath, he blurted out,

"I'm a single bloke who lives alone. My mother died twelve months ago, and an aunt stayed for a while. I'm trying to say I have a large house, and you're welcome to share it. The bathroom door has a lock on it, and if you are nervous, you can shove a chair under the bedroom door handle."

Jacqui narrowed her eyes and struggled to gauge the stranger's intentions.

"What do you get out of this offer?"

Brett rushed on, stumbling over his words.

"Ah, well, can you cook the odd meal or help with the cleaning as part of the agreement? I'm running the farm alone, and getting everything done is hard."

"So, you're telling me you want a housekeeper?"

Jacqui watched with fascination as a flush crept across the man's face, and he chewed on his cheek.

"No, I want company."

Jacqui scrutinised him. Standing closer, she could see that her first impression of his build was correct, but now that his face was visible, she recognised an earnestness in his expression that resonated with her. He looked dishevelled, but the straightforward way he presented the offer made her decide.

"I don't have lots of options. Hell, that sounds ungrateful. I apologise; I didn't mean to be rude. It's been a long day. Thanks, I accept the offer. Can the details wait until later? I'm tired and hungry; I only want food and a bed tonight."

Ten kilometres of dirt road later, Jacqui followed Brett's ute into the driveway of a big Queenslander-style home. The drive had given her plenty of time to worry about her choice. Might it have been safer to drive back to Lonsdale tonight and find accommodation in the light of day tomorrow? Brett would not be a suspect if she disappeared without a trace because no one knew they were together. She thought, Get hold of yourself; this guy is different from the uncouth louts at the pub. If he gave her any cause for concern tonight, Jacqui could barricade the bedroom door. She could find an alternative tomorrow if she weren't comfortable, even if she had to drive to Lonsdale.

The house was shabby from the outside and needed a coat of paint. Brett led the way into a tired-looking kitchen and moved newspapers and other paraphernalia from the chairs.

"Why don't you point me to the bedroom I can use? Put the kettle on, please. I'm desperate for a cuppa."

"Ah, sure. That's a good idea," said Brett as he led her into the hallway. He pointed to the first door. "My bedroom is here. You're welcome to use my parents' room. It's at the back of the house and has a small bathroom attached."

"You don't mind me using that room?"

"No, leaving the biggest room in the house empty is senseless. Put your stuff in there, and I'll find sheets."

Brett fossicked around in a cupboard and pulled out an armful of linen. Laden with clean-smelling sheets, pillowcases and towels, he walked back to the bedroom and set them on the bed.

"Now for the food," he said.

When Jacqui entered the kitchen, she looked around the room. It had been a long time since the kitchen had seen a mop or broom. She opened the pantry door and discovered a can of mushrooms, a packet of pasta, and a container of flour.

"Not much in there. That's why I was in town. I wanted to eat at the pub, but your arrival interrupted that."

"There's a can of mushroom and a packet of pasta here. Are there any eggs?" Jacqui asked.

"Hm," looking in the fridge, he said, "Yep, there are two and a piece of bacon. There's bread, but it's not fresh."

Jacqui mixed the ingredients to make a mock egg and bacon pie and served it with the pasta. The circumstances they found themselves in were awkward. They were strangers with no common interests, so they ate the meal silently. Jacqui asked a few questions about the district and the school, but Brett's replies were short and to the point. She gazed around the room as she ate. The kitchen showed signs of neglect. Why does a robust, healthy bloke let his home fall into such disrepair? She gave a mental shrug and finished her meal in silence. With a pain pounding at her temples, Jacqui put her dishes on the bench.

"I have a dreadful headache. I need to go to bed. Leave the dishes on the bench, and I'll wash them in the morning. Goodnight."

"Um, yeah, sure. Good night."

Fate delivered A nice-looking girl into his home, and he could not talk to her. Brett watched her leave the kitchen, disgusted with his pathetic attempt at conversation. What must she think of him? It had been so long since he had a dinner companion that his social skills were rusty. He vowed to do better when he saw her in the morning.

# Chapter Seven

B rett woke for the first time in many months, feeling buoyant. The thought of another person in the house gave him a shot of energy. It had been ages since he had started the day with enthusiasm. He vowed to make his border more welcoming and to engage her in conversation.

Before Jacqui arrived, he went through the motions, but now another person was living here; he should try. After a quick shower, he went to start breakfast. He recalled that there was nothing to eat, so he filled the kettle and loaded the toaster with bread.

"Mmm, coffee smells good," said Jacqui as she entered the kitchen.

"Didn't you want me to cook?"

In the light of day, Brett realised she was taller than he had first thought. Her short dark hair framed her high cheekbones. Her jeans were firm enough to hug her long legs and the generous curves of her bottom. She had blue eyes framed by long, thick lashes. Her skin, devoid of makeup, gave her a wholesome, natural look. Not wanting Jacqui to catch him staring, he averted his gaze. After dealing with Aunt Gloria, he reminded himself that if it looks too good to be true, it doubtless is. He planned to enter this agreement with caution.

"If you cook dinner, I can fix breakfast. Sorry, there's only toast and coffee. We should shop this morning."

There were a few awkward moments; Jacqui wasn't sure if she should help or wait at the table. Brett solved the problem by saying,

"Do you mind buttering the toast? There might be a jar of jam or Vegemite in the pantry." She hunted in the pantry and came up with an empty jar of Vegemite and some crystallised honey.

"The shopping list should start with Vegemite and honey," she laughed.

Over breakfast, Brett's nerves settled, and the two exchanged information. Jacqui explained why she was in the country, and Brett related his struggles with the farm. Although they had just met, Jacqui liked the tall, solitary farmer. Now that he had relaxed, he was easy to talk to and didn't take offence at her reluctance to live in a rural location.

"What do you want to do today? Do we shop this morning or this afternoon? If you are busy with school, you can pick up something from the café for dinner and leave buying food until tomorrow."

"I need to collect the key to the school building and see if the runaway teacher left any notes or had work prepared. Do you want my presence in your house to stay private?"

"Let's keep our arrangement under wraps for the minute. The other blokes will have a field day when they hear you're staying here. The grub that runs the pub doesn't deserve to know what's happening."

"There is a week of school holidays left for teachers, so I can help in the house when I've sorted the school work. If you have time one day during the week, can we go somewhere to buy a car? Dad helped me get the little Corolla, but I doubt he'll drive up here to help me buy another car. It pains me to admit it, but I need something more practical."

Brett laughed. "It's a snazzy little car for the city, but out here, it will fall apart in six months."

He stacked the dishes in the sink and grabbed his hat.

"I must make a move; I need to feed the cattle. After morning tea, we can go shopping."

"How do you feed the cows? Do you have feed drums or something?" Jacqui asked.

He laughed. "Hey, city girl, you need to call them cattle. Cattle farmers can have cows, steers, heifers, bulls, calves, or bullocks. They'll laugh at you if you tell the locals I have cows. There are no feed drums; I drive into the paddock and push the feed off at regular intervals. I keep moving and stopping until I lay out all the feed."

"Why don't you have someone to help?"

"I can't afford to pay anyone, so I must do it myself."

"I'm not in a hurry to go into town, and I can drive a manual car. If I drive, you can tell me where to stop. Ah, that's if you want a hand," she said.

Brett grinned at her. "That's great. Grab a hat and shoes," he said, looking at her thongs.

Jacqui struggled with the gearshift on the old ute. Brett opened the gate to the first paddock, and as she drove through, he closed it and jumped onto the back. As Jacqui drove, Brett cut the string on the hay bale and tossed it overboard once in sight of the cattle. He directed Jacqui to turn left towards the second gate, and as she halted, he jumped off again and repeated the actions he had just completed in the first paddock. There were three more gateways and paddocks, and Brett signalled her to stop. She pulled up, and he climbed into the cabin.

"Are we finished?"

With a huge grin, he said,

"Yep, and that's a job that, by myself, takes half of the morning. Your help has made it that much faster. That's outstanding. Thanks."

Jacqui laughed, "Well, if that's all there is to it, this farming stuff looks simple. Who knows, I might make a country girl yet." Brett just raised his eyebrows at her.

Brett and Jacqui had a shower and a quick cup of tea. They decided not to drive two cars into town to put the locals off the scent. They took Jacqui's car because Brett thought they might get a good deal in Lonsdale. It would be easier if they could get a trade-in price today and an immediate changeover.

The first stop was the post office to pick up the school keys. A bell rang as Jacqui pushed the door open, and the woman at the counter lifted her head. The building inside was constructed with tongue-and-groove panels, and the benches appeared to have been in place for centuries. Despite the place's outdated interior, it seemed to run efficiently. New computers balanced on the serving counters, and bright displays adorned the walls.

The shop assistant had tied her blond hair with a scarf, and her glasses were perched on the bridge of her nose. A tight pair of jeans and a shirt did nothing to flatter the overweight woman, but she smiled as Jacqui walked toward her.

"Hello, darl, you must be the new schoolteacher we expected. We thought you'd arrive yesterday."

"Yes, I'm a new teacher. My name is Jacqui Stuart. It was late when I arrived yesterday, and you had closed."

"I'm Beth Thompson. I half expected to have to give you a bed last night, but you made other arrangements, I guess."

"Well, I wish I'd known. The only place still open when I got here was the pub. All I got were insults and lewd propositions."

"That sounds normal. That pub is not a suitable place for a woman to frequent. I guess you want the school keys. The other bloke shot out of here fast when the Department notified him of your appointment. He was eager to leave, and no one was sad to see him go. He never fitted in here; the parents weren't happy, and the kids disliked him."

"Great, I have a public relations disaster to fix."

Jacqui walked the two blocks to the school. It surprised her how secluded it was despite its proximity to the shops. Large gum trees screened it from the other buildings, and the rear of the block appeared to be native scrub. Large shrubs crowded the walkways, and branches hung over the paths.

The school buildings came into view. One structure appeared to be the original building. It was wooden and raised on stumps; a small front porch sheltered the entry. The building was in such poor condition that it had been unused for many years. Its windows were grimy and covered in cobwebs, and the weatherboards were peeling. Corrugated roofing sheets had come loose. Jacqui was reluctant to check inside and was glad that Brett arrived just then.

"This looks like a haunted house, not a schoolroom," she said.

"Yeah, it's grim. I must admit I don't drive past here often. Let's take a quick look in here and then check out the rest of the school. This building looks as though it is unused."

Jacqui walked onto the porch and hunted through the bundle of keys Beth had given her. She found a large, rusty key and inserted it into the lock. The key grated as it turned in the lock. When she pushed the door open, the stench that escaped from the room was overpowering. She reeled back and gagged.

"Oh my God," said Brett. "That smells as though dead bodies are rotting in there. That is putrid!"

Jacqui held her handkerchief over her nose.

"Now I know why it's unused. I'll have to get the Education Department to decontaminate and clean that room." Struggling with the odour, she pulled the door closed and locked it.

They inspected the other room and discovered it was a poorly maintained double demountable. The schoolrooms and the two small offices were dirty, and the carpet required repair. Technology in the classrooms stretched to nothing more than chalkboards. A check of the toilet block showed a level of sanitation that wouldn't be acceptable in a hut. The final straw was the playground, with knee-high grass covering the entire place.

"So much to do, so little time," Brett quipped.

Jacqui shook her head from side to side. She had never seen a school so substandard in her teaching career. The conditions were circa 1920, and teaching the national curriculum was impossible without technological aid. How could the Department provide such a poor-quality educational experience for the children?

"Let's go and buy a car. This mess will take me days to sort out, involving thousands of phone calls and emails. If we do the car and the shopping, I can spend the next week trying to get the Education Department to do something," said Jacqui.

The trip to Lonsdale, with Brett driving, was less harrowing than her first trip. There were fewer trucks during this trip, and Brett was better at moving to the shoulder to prevent being sideswiped.

"This is one road I hope not to travel often. How do the trucks manage to force everyone else off the road? Where are the police when you need them?" Jacqui asked.

"The trucks are the livelihood of the district, so nobody wants to anger them. They are more cautious if they see a police car, but a police car here is a rarity."

Once in Lonsdale, Brett took Jacqui to a car dealer he knew, and together they picked out a small SUV. She looked at her little car, remembering the excitement she had felt when she purchased it. Her dad and Brett correctly assessed its unsuitability for the rough country roads, but that didn't dispel her sadness.

The next port of call was the supermarket she had passed the day before. The shop served the large town, stocking most essential items. When it came time to pay for the trolley full of groceries, Jacqui pulled out a card to complete their purchase. Stowing the groceries away, they loaded the back of the new SUV to capacity.

As they drove back to Manwarring, Brett broached the subject of money.

"Jacqui, seeing as you can't escape the car for the next hour, we should discuss money."

"Okay, I guess we need to come up with a price for rent and electricity. How much were you thinking?"

"If you looked around the house this morning, you could tell things are tough. I'm living on a line of credit and grants from the government, which I have to pay back." He ran one hand through his hair.

"When I offered accommodation, I never considered the costs, such as food. If I had to do the shopping today, I'd have bought a few frozen dinners and called it quits."

"Please say you're not having second thoughts," Jacqui pleaded.

"Well, yes and no. Hell, this situation is embarrassing! I can't afford to pay my share of the food you bought today, and I can't expect you to live on frozen dinners," he explained.

"Could part of the payment be with the groceries I buy each week? If we do that, we get to eat, and I still have somewhere to stay. Does it matter if the payment is in cash or groceries?"

"I guess it doesn't matter. Are you happy with that?"

"Yes, I can't see any problem," said Jacqui.

# Chapter Eight

As they drove back into Manwarring in her new SUV, Jacqui thanked her lucky stars for Brett's presence in this country living experience. After spending the last two weeks at her parents' home meeting humourless, self-important men, it was refreshing to realise Brett was a nice guy. God knows where she might be without his accommodation offer and help to buy the car.

"Can we stop at school before we go home?"

"Yes, but when we leave, you need to drive."

Jacqui grimaced. The prospect of driving on the dirt road to his house didn't excite Jacqui, but she could see the logic in his suggestion. Once they arrived outside the school, she hunted for her new digital camera in the glove box. Many photos later, they were ready to go home.

"Tomorrow, I'll start my battle with the education department. I'll simultaneously hit the district office, regional office, head office, the local member and the education minister."

"Wow, don't let me get on your wrong side! You'd bury me under a mountain of letters."

"We have only two weeks' holiday left. I start work next week; the kids begin a week later. Nobody should come back to that mess. Who is the cleaner? Is there a grounds person? Is there a teacher aide?"

"Whoa. As far as I know, you are the only staff member. Beth might be able to answer your questions about what goes on at the school. Try asking her."

After unloading the shopping, Brett left Jacqui to her own devices while he finished the outside jobs. She decided that, as he had been living on sandwiches and tins of spaghetti, a roast would be easy to make, and she was sure Brett would appreciate a cooked meal. After the meat was cooked, she peeled potatoes and carrots, cut the pumpkin and beans, and placed the prepared vegetables in a bowl of water.

With her hands on her hips, she surveyed the mass of papers and paraphernalia that had taken up lodging on the table and chairs. A few documents looked significant, and Brett had screwed up those he didn't need. Newspapers from weeks ago were on the floor next to a chair, and pieces of hose and other mechanical gear were on the table. Jacqui found garbage bags and sorted the bits and pieces that littered the table. She put the essential-looking papers in the office, the rubbish into the big wheelie bin outside, and the mechanical stuff at the back door for Brett to move to the shed. Now that she had cleared the tabletop, she located the cleaning detergents and scrubbed the table.

She raided the linen cupboard and looked for a tablecloth. Once the cloth was in place and the cutlery and utensils were on the table, she put the vegetables in the oven to cook. After contemplating the profusion of cookware, plates and cutlery in the sink, she ran hot, soapy water and started washing up. The dishes in and around the tub were easy to clean, but Jacqui needed to scrub some things. She put the pots with hard-to-shift stains in the laundry sink to soak.

Jacqui checked the time and decided she had enough time to sweep and wash the kitchen floor. The floor, covered with grime, needed mopping twice, but the results were worth the effort. The lovely marble tiles complemented the wooden cupboards and pine benchtops, creating a warm, comfortable atmosphere in the kitchen.

Hot, sweaty and smelly, Jacqui showered. Aware of the drought conditions, she had a quick shower. While drying off, the screen door banged shut. She pulled on jeans and a shirt and walked back to the kitchen. Brett stopped mid-stride, a bark of laughter bursting from his mouth.

"You sure know how to take a guy by surprise. This room looks remarkable, and that's a roast cooking if I'm not wrong."

"I decided that a good meal was in order after eating toast for breakfast and fast food for lunch. Besides, you have been living on tinned spaghetti and sandwiches, haven't you?"

Brett grinned and nodded.

"Guilty as charged. Will dinner be ruined if I take a quick shower?"

Half an hour later, they sat at the table. While Brett carved the roast lamb, Jacqui searched the fridge and found the wine she had purchased. As they worked their way through the meal, she asked many questions about the farm.

"I have another question. Tell me to mind my business if I'm out of order, but why don't you have domestic animals?"

"What animals do you mean?"

"There is room for a chook shed. You could have a milking cow or chooks. You have no working dogs and no cats. I thought all farms had working dogs and cats."

"I've lost interest in the farm and am considering selling. It's lonely here by myself, and as I grew up without domestic animals, it never occurred to me to get any animals after Mum died. Dad said dogs were more trouble than they're worth, and Mum had no interest in chooks or a milking cow, but she had splendid gardens. The mowed area at the front was a garden, and the large patch of weeds on the side was her vegetable patch. I don't have the time or the interest to weed and grow anything in them."

"Are you still considering selling, or now you have company? Will you stay?" asked Jacqui.

"Please understand me; your company is great. It doesn't solve the need for another farmhand I can't afford to pay."

"Why not get a few working dogs? You only need to feed them once you've outlaid the purchase price. If we go online, there might be someone who can help us learn the skills and where to find the dogs. Working dogs would relieve the need for another pair of hands, and if you need hands sometimes, I could help."

Brett looked sceptical, but once Jacqui had an idea, she was hard to stop. They did the dishes in companionable silence and then moved to the office to use the computer. They discussed the possibilities, and then Brett sent an e-mail to the rescue man, a breeder and someone who sold dogs. A search online revealed that dogs without extended pedigrees sold for as little as $300, and there were shelters for rescued working dogs.

"Let's see if any of those are options."

"Can you help with my stuff? I need these photos uploaded into a file, and then I'll back up the e-mails by sending hard copies to each person. People can say they didn't get an e-mail, but it's much tougher to say the letter didn't arrive either."

Jacqui composed what she hoped were non-threatening letters to alert the offices to the appalling conditions at the school. She highlighted the lack of technology—the cornerstone of the national curriculum—and of support staff. She wanted the equipment to make it easier if she were the only teacher in a two-teacher school.

# Chapter Nine

The following day began the same as the day before, but breakfast was far more substantial now that they'd done the shopping. After a cooked meal, they went out to feed the stock. Jacqui grinned as she maneuvered the ute without stalling it and only occasionally crunched the gears. Brett cringed each time she ground the gears, but her help meant they finished before morning tea, so he didn't complain. With the job completed, he looked at Jacqui and said,

"Ok, farm girl, where do you want the chook shed?"

"Why don't we reconnoitre the yard for safety and ease of access?"

He threw his head back and laughed. "Nobody uses a word like reconnoitre unless they're in a war movie."

"Stick around, buster, and I'll improve your vocab."

They chose a location on the other side of what had been the vegetable garden for the hen house, then returned to the house to work out the design of the enclosure and the nesting boxes.

Once they agreed on the blueprint for their coop, Brett worked out the cost of the materials needed for construction. Even with taking shortcuts, the amount was more than he could afford. Though she had known him briefly, Jacqui could tell he was worried about the cost and offered to pay for the new pen and the laying hens herself.

"You might have to pay for dogs since the coop is my idea. Let me pay for the materials and the chooks."

He looked ready to decline the offer and then stared at her.

"What happens when you leave?"

She laughed, "I promise I'll give you full custody of the chooks and not ask for any profits from the eggs. OK?"

He smiled. "Thank God I ran out of food when you arrived in town. If I had anything in the pantry to eat, I wouldn't have gone to the pub for dinner, and I wouldn't have met you."

When they arrived in town, Brett dropped Jacqui off at the post office and continued to the hardware and feed shed. She needed to talk to Beth about the school and see if she knew anything about other staff.

"Caught yourself a good one, did you?" Beth said as soon as Jacqui entered the shop.

"Pardon?"

"You and young Brett. It didn't take you long to latch onto him, did it?"

"Wow, talk about offensive! Is this how small towns work? There was no latching onto anybody. I'm boarding with Brett, seeing as no one else had genuine offers. And not that it is anyone else's business, but I'm in my bedroom and ensuite, so everything is legitimate. Maybe you'd like to spread that through the town."

"This is a small town; everyone knows everyone else's business. You're sleeping in his parents' room, then?"

"You're familiar with the house, so, yes, I'm using his mother's room. I was hoping you could help. The school is in appalling condition; did the other teacher ever receive any maintenance? Is there a teacher's aide, a gardener, or a cleaner?"

"You're not in the city now, Luv. There's nobody else, only you. I believe the other bloke tried but got nowhere."

"Well, there's no way that place is up to scratch; the playground isn't safe. What do the kids do? Do they remove the snakes from the cricket pitch before they play?"

Beth shrugged. "It's always been that way."

"I may be a city girl, but it's obvious that the Department is short-changing the students with the lack of equipment and second-rate buildings. Things must change when the grade sevens go to high school next year. The kids will not be ready unless the parents have an internet connection to the national curriculum."

After talking to Beth, Jacqui walked toward the feed store to join Brett. She glanced at the road and crossed. She was thinking of the things that needed fixing and wondered if anyone in the town would volunteer to help.

"Oi, ya stuck-up bitch, watch where you're walking."

Jacqui jumped back as a beat-up Land Cruiser ground to a halt next to her.

"Just because you're sleeping with that Sanderson fellow doesn't give you the right to wander all over the roads."

She recognised her abuser as a drinker from the pub and was almost sure he was the one who offered her accommodation with benefits. She wanted to flip him off, but being a professional, she ignored him. "I'm talking to you, girlie," he shouted.

Although rarely upset by an altercation with a motorist, the verbal assault unnerved her. She thought this man was one nasty customer and vowed to keep a low profile when he was around.

With the ute loaded up, they drove back to the farm. Jacqui started calling the school authorities. She contacted all the officers she had informed Brett about and supported each call with an email. The emails included an attachment with photos of the school and playground. Each e-mail requested a speedy response, as school was due to resume in less than two weeks. She knew how the politics in these offices worked, so she followed the e-mails with a printed copy of the correspondence and photos. She addressed the mail to the CEO of each department and registered them as a safeguard.

Happy to have finished the e-mails and letters, she turned her attention to cleaning the lounge room. When Brett arrived for dinner, a tired-looking Jacqui greeted him.

"What did you do this afternoon? You looked exhausted!"

"I am tired but pleased with myself. I finished the phone calls, e-mails and letters to the department's admin officers and cleaned the lounge room!"

"Don't wear yourself out. I didn't offer you a board so you could work yourself to death."

"I hope I'm not overstepping the mark, but I want to organise the house before school starts. It will take ages to sort through the kids' work, or, as I suspect, their lack thereof. Oh, I want to ask you something."

"No, we cannot have camels," said Brett with a grin.

"It's much easier than that. Is there a room available for me to study? If there's a desk here, I won't need to carry stuff backwards and forwards to school."

"Sure. This house has three bedrooms that we don't use. Take your pick. The shed might have a desk, although it will need cleaning. I'll look for you tomorrow."

As Brett lay in bed that night, he was thankful for Jacqui's presence. He was ready to admit defeat when she walked into his life. The loneliness of farming now that his mother was no longer there was unbearable. He was an isolated and unhappy man with no family left, and his few close friends were moving to live in the city. He felt burdened by everyday decisions and only did the jobs he couldn't avoid. Jacqui's occupancy had changed so much in the last few days. Working with her in the morning and eating meals each evening felt right. She eased the tension that attacked him daily, and her sense of humour lightened up the atmosphere in the house. He hoped that her placement at the school would last for years to come.

A small thought nagged at him. Was this too good to be true? Jacqui seemed genuine and without ulterior motives. She was feisty and energetic, and she made him laugh. It was hard to be unaffected by her enthusiasm for life, but he worried he was already getting in too deep. His admiration for her could be his undoing.

# Chapter Ten

Jacqui and Brett had spent hours browsing online for working dogs. There was a lot of information, but Jacqui hadn't convinced Brett that a dog was the answer to his problems. His concern was if he ran into trouble handling a dog, whom could he ask for help? If he bought a working dog, he needed a mentor. How does a person find a tutor?

"With my lack of experience with dogs, a puppy is not an option. These working dogs are smart, so a puppy could learn many bad habits before I learned anything," Brett said.

There were numerous options online and a wealth of information, which caused his enthusiasm to waver. It was all too hard. If not for Jacqui pushing, he would have put the decision in the too-hard basket. As they tried to make sense of the information, she watched him become immersed in details and doubts. When Brett sagged into the chair and rubbed his temples, Jacqui felt a wave of remorse. She scolded herself for pushing him into deciding his future. She sat next to him and reached for his hand.

"Brett, look at me."

He raised his head and gave a stiff smile. He threaded his fingers through hers.

"You must think I'm a terrible wimp. I'm scared to change how I do things, although a glance around here will show you that the old ways aren't working."

She sighed as she ran a hand through her short, wavy hair.

"We always had dogs when I was a kid. I know they can help ease stress, are good listeners and don't judge. If they get attention and food, they're happy. I understand that getting a dog is an enormous leap of faith for you. The farm is yours; you need to decide, not let me push you into changing things. If you aren't ready for this, say so. I promise to stop nagging. Sometimes, I get carried away with an idea, so I'm sorry if you feel pressured. We can shelve the plan or put it on hold, whichever suits you best.

He gazed over at her.

"How did I get this lucky? Your presence here challenges me to be brave and try different things. Let's review the information and decide who to talk to." He squeezed her hand back and sat up straight in his chair. She could tell he had temporarily set aside his doubts, and they could move forward to improve his situation.

"Why not chat with the man who runs the dog rescue centre?"

Jacqui left him alone in the office while he chatted with the refugee owner. She knew the place was a privately run affair from her online search and hoped the owner would support a newcomer to the skill.

"Hey, Jac, we're in business. The guy sounds genuine and has offered to be available to discuss any problems that arise, even if I decide not to take one of his dogs. I want to organise an appointment to meet him."

Brett appeared to be taking his time, and Jacqui was impatient and excited. He grinned at her; she was a whirlwind who dragged you with her.

"Let's go!" she urged

After many phone calls, today was the day they could see a rescue working dog in action. Her eyes sparkled, and she wore a huge grin. She wriggled nonstop in her seat and fidgeted with the seat belt and the radio. They had a two-hour drive, and Brett thought she might explode before arriving at the refuge.

"Calm down, woman. Brett said that this dog mightn't be the right one, and you'll be disappointed," Brett said.

"The sooner we leave, the sooner we'll know," she replied.

The drive was endless, and the scenery was uninspiring. Jacqui decided that, having seen one drought-stricken farm, you'd seen them all. As far as she could tell, the land was bare and barren of grass.

Scrawny-looking cattle stood in dispirited groups under the trees' slight shade.

"Don't all farmers feed their stock? Your animals are fatter than these are."

"When the money runs out, and the cattle are too weak to make the trip to the market, there's not much you can do. I'd shoot a few to give the others a chance, but how would you cope if you destroyed half of the herd and rain came the next week? They hang on and hope."

After a quick snack at a small cafe, the travellers set out on the last leg of the journey. The rescue centre was on the outskirts of Lonsdale, and they expected to arrive just before lunchtime. Brett turned into the entrance and negotiated the pitted dirt driveway. The place was old but well-maintained, and numerous sheds were scattered around the property's outskirts. As they pulled up, Jacqui grabbed his hand.

"You know there's no pressure to decide today. If you're not sure, we can always come back."

When they met at the front of the car, he pulled her into a quick hug. "This is the first major change I've made since Mum died. Thanks for the encouragement."

The noise of barking dogs heralded their arrival, and an older man came out of the house.

"G' day. You must be Brett. I'm Sid Newland," said the man.

"Hi, Sid; it's nice to meet you. I'd like you to meet Jacqui, a friend of mine."

After shaking hands, Sid looked to be appraising the young couple. When he nodded, it was clear that he had decided.

"You said you've never worked with dogs, eh? What's the interest in learning now?"

"Well, the dog was Jacqui's idea; that's why she's here today. My mother passed away twelve months ago, and I need help on the farm with the cattle. There's no money to pay a worker, so maybe a dog will do the trick," Brett said.

"I have two dogs that might suit. Come and see what you think."

They followed Sid as he walked toward a set of kennels hidden behind the sheds. The well-designed enclosures looked new. There was a sheltered place for the dogs to protect them from the weather, and the runs were roomy and clean. After hearing the people's approach, the dogs inside the kennels ran to the gate. There were four dogs in the kennels. Jacqui recognised two of the dogs; they were border collies. Sid recounted the dogs' breeding history. The other two dogs were trickier than the first two. One might be a kelpie, but the other dog had her baffled. Sid opened the kennel gate so they could enter. He followed them into the run and gave a command. The dogs stopped fussing and dropped to the ground.

The stories of the three dogs were similar. All the older dogs had owners who didn't see the need to reward elderly dogs for years of work; euthanising them was more straightforward. The fourth dog was a puppy that Sid rescued from a cruel owner and spent the last few months training. While he talked to Brett and Jacqui, the dogs waited patiently for him to release them. He released each dog one at a time so Jacqui and Brett could handle them.

Brett scrutinised both the puppy and the nondescript dog. "One of these two would be my pick."

Sid laughed, saying, "You might not have worked with dogs before, son, but you have a decent eye. You chose the two I thought might suit you. You'll need to make accommodations for Barney's age; put him on the motorbike or your quad bike as you go out to get the cattle, but once there, he'll work a treat. The pup, Mollie, shows much potential and will make a top worker with Barney's steadying influence."

Once they decided, they followed Sid to the house for lunch and discussed how to care for the dogs. Curious for answers, Jacqui said, "Sid, what breed is Barney? He looks like a bitser. Is there a pedigree there?"

"Yep, he's a heeler cross kelpie. Great dogs, those; they'll work till they drop."

While they ate lunch, Jacqui marvelled at the wealth of information the older man possessed. This man's lone battle to help the district's working dogs touched her heart. Jacqui took notes on the hints Sid gave Brett about caring for and handling the dogs. He suggested they drop both dogs off at the vet's: Barney for a check-up and Molly for neutering. Sis also gave Brett a list of the commands most commonly used and tips on bedding and securing dogs at night.

"No point in having an entire female on the place. It brings in all the stray dogs. You end up with pups, and the bitch can't work. When the time comes to replace Barney, you'll be an old hand at this, and breeders have plenty of young' uns."

When they came to discuss the price of the dogs, Jacqui realised, with surprise, that Brett had a stubborn streak. Happy to place the dogs in a loving home, Sid didn't want payment. Brett insisted on paying what he thought was a fair price. Jacqui watched on as the two men battled for recognition of their viewpoint. With no immediate victor in sight, she interrupted.

"Sid, if you let Brett pay, you can rescue more dogs. Trained dogs are far more expensive. A puppy would cost $300–$400 if we were to purchase it from a breeder. Please let us help you with your work here."

Sid chuckled and watched Brett. "Now I know why you brought her with you, son; she fights dirty. Okay, Missy, I'll concede, but only because you asked nicely. How's an old bloke supposed to fight against a determined female?"

While the men loaded the dogs into the cattle crate on the back of the ute, Jacqui rang the vet in Lonsdale to book an appointment. They were ready to leave, finances aside, with lists of tips in hand. Brett and Sid shook hands, but Jacqui hugged the older man. "Keep up the good work. We'll be in touch."

# Chapter Eleven

With the dog problem sorted, Jacqui decided it was time to push for action on the school repairs and the extra-staff budget. There was little response to the letters and e-mails. Her phone calls resulted in officers and ministers being too busy to speak to her. There was no point in visiting the various departments that handled repairs; if they refused to talk to her on the phone, they would balk at speaking with her in person. She knew she would eventually have to take the fight to the department.

A snobby-sounding receptionist answered her first call and said the Minister was too busy to speak with Jacqui. Her anger flared, but she strove to reply civilly.

"I'm sorry; have you informed the Minister that I wish to speak to him? Has he received my e-mail?"

"Oh dear, the email must have gone into the junk mailbox. We delete messages from unknown sources."

"Then I'm glad I sent a hard copy of the letter. It's unlikely that there was a disaster with Australia Post, so a letter should have arrived just after the e-mail," Jacqui said through gritted teeth.

"I'm unsure if the Minister has found the time to read your letter."

"I'll wait while you relay a message to the Minister; either he takes the time to read and respond now, or he can read the letter in tomorrow's newspaper."

"Are you threatening the Minister?"

"Certainly not! However, most public servants read the paper in the morning to stay informed about important issues. I promise to make it easier for the Minister to read by including many photos for the journalists to use."

The receptionist slammed the phone down, and Jacqui heard the sound of heels clicking across the floor and a door opening. The phone clicked a minute later, and a male voice said, "Can I help you, Miss Stuart?"

"Mr White, I have sent you both a letter and an e-mail. Your receptionist said she deleted the e-mail as junk mail, so thank God for Australia Post. I require immediate and severe action regarding the two-teacher school at Manwarring. The school is in an unbelievable state of disrepair; there is no internet, and the toilet facilities are unsanitary."

"It is not within my power to convince the department to upgrade a school. This request must go through the correct channels, which takes time. You should contact your local member, and he might lobby on your behalf," Mr White said.

"Sir, I have contacted you, our local member, the district office, and the regional office. I can't get anyone to commit to helping with the school's repairs. Nobody has shown any interest at all. The district's children are due to start school in a week, but the rooms are unsafe, the playground is a snake haven, and the toilet block is a health hazard. If I am the only teacher in a two-teacher school, I need a budget that allows me to hire a teacher aide."

"I'm sorry, miss, I can't help. Contact your local representative and request the necessary paperwork from the district office. Once you have applied, we will assess whether we can incorporate some improvements this financial year. If not, we will have to wait until next year when we can include the repairs in the budget. Good day to you."

Jacqui sat holding the beeping phone; he had hung up on her. She drummed her fingers on the desk as she considered the options. While going to the media was a choice, not trying other options first might cause the department to transfer her to Timbuktu. While this would never be easy, she hoped to receive a response. Jacqui flipped through the local phone book and found the council office's phone number. She spoke to a friendly, efficient-sounding receptionist who informed her that the mayor had an opening in his schedule for the next day. Jacqui provided her details and the reason for the meeting, then asked the receptionist to schedule an appointment.

The next afternoon, she left the mayor's office with her fists clenched in frustration. While he did meet with her, his response was as cynical as theirs. Hold a working bee, he said. She tried to explain that while a farmer with a slasher might come and cut the grass, nobody could afford to pay for the new carpet, build a toilet block, or fumigate the old building. Although he expressed his support, he was unhelpful, leaving Jacqui unsure about what to do.

Over dinner that night, Jacqui shared with Brett the responses she had received from each administrator and minister she had contacted. Contacting the media was the last resort; Jacqui feared she might get the school problems sorted and be transferred out of the district.

"If you can't go to the media, why not contact the shadow ministers of the opposition party? Your political affiliations don't matter; the shadow ministry will jump on this to discredit the government."

"Do you think the shadow minister for Education will be interested?"

"Don't just talk to the Education Minister. You need to include the Health Minister; those toilets are atrocious. While you're at it, why don't you ask them to visit the school and bring someone involved in Main Roads with them? After they travel the road from Lonsdale, we might get repairs or upgrades done."

"Good thinking! I can start with more emails tonight. I'll do the same as the government ministers; send e-mails and follow up with letters and hard copies of the photos."

In her home office, Jacqui found the details of the shadow cabinet. With their names and office details at hand, she sent the communications to the various ministers. She included a copy of the response letters from the government ministers.

While Jacqui played with the dogs, Brett worked on the farm's financials. Although she knew she shouldn't play with the dogs, the temptation was too much.

The phone rang, interrupting Brett's concentration.

"Bugger." He dived for the phone.

"Hello, sorry. Who is this?" A moment later, clarity hit; the phone call was for Jacqui.

"Jac! There's a phone call," he shouted from the back door. Jacqui jogged up from the shed and shot a query at him. He shrugged and handed her the phone.

"Hi, Jacqui Stuart speaking." She waved at Brett, signalling him to stay and listen. "My appointment was from the first day of the third term, but the teacher here took stress leave. I started work earlier, but the kids don't return to school for another week. Friday? Sure, that would be great. What time do I expect you? Okay. Thanks very much. Bye." Jacqui clicked off the phone, let out a whoop of joy, and then did a happy dance. Brett laughed and said,

"I assume that was someone important, and they are coming to check out the school?"

"Yes, and yes! The shadow minister for education, the Health Minister, a financial expert, and an engineer from Main Roads will be here at ten o'clock. They will inspect the school and determine if they can assist in resolving the funding issues. After all the knockbacks, I hope these guys are more useful than others I've met. Can we eat lunch here? I might throw together a few salads."

"If you want to get meat from the freezer, I'll clean off the Barbie. We can have salads with the steaks."

"You are such a treasure," Jacqui said, planting a big kiss on his cheek. Colour rushed across Brett's cheeks, and she felt awkward, having let her enthusiasm run away with her. She shrugged her shoulders and shuffled her feet.

"Sorry; sometimes I get carried away."

Brett laughed. "That's okay; just warn me next time so I can take full advantage of your enthusiasm." He winked at her, his blue eyes sparkling with laughter, and then he disappeared outside to clean the barbecue

Jacqui slapped her hands against her cheeks as she watched him walk away. She saw new facets of his personality as she spent time with him. This playful, suggestive side was not one she had seen before, and she had to admit that she had enjoyed the innuendo he had thrown at her.

Jacqui raced out to her SUV. She was running late. Time seemed to get away; now, it was a rush to be on time to meet the shadow cabinet ministers visiting to inspect the school. When she threw her bag into the passenger seat, she realised the vehicle was leaning. She hurried around to check the car's passenger side and, with dismay, saw a flat tyre on the front wheel.

"No!" she groaned, grabbing her bag to race back to the house.

"Brett, my front tyre is flat. Can I take your ute? I don't have time to change the tyre; I'm running late."

"Sure, and while you're gone, I'll change it."

As Jacqui stood at the school's gateway, she watched the very dusty sedan pull up. She bounced from foot to foot, her excitement hard to contain. Someone was paying attention to her complaints, and with relief, she realised this visit might set the plans for the repairs in motion.

After a moment, the doors opened, and the men, all dressed in impeccable suits, climbed out of the vehicle. They approached Jacqui, introduced themselves, and stated their portfolios. The engineer from Main Roads, Sam, said to her,

"That is, without doubt, the worst and most dangerous highway I ever had the misfortune to travel. Is it always like that?"

"Yes, which is why I was glad to find somewhere to board just out of town. The trucks ignore other traffic, forcing cars off the road and overtaking in unsafe places."

The shadow minister for education, Tony, said,

"Okay, let's see the buildings, and we'll take more photos to add weight to yours."

For the next hour, the group walked through the buildings. Jacqui showed them the workplace health and safety issues, substandard seating arrangements, and lack of technology. She turned on the fans to let the men hear the noise they made, which was so intrusive that they remained unused during any active teaching. Each minister made lists relevant to their portfolio and thoroughly scrutinised the main building. When Jacqui showed them the toilet blocks, they shuddered at the primitive conditions.

Finally, she took them to the old building, and before opening the door, she said, "I must warn you, the odour that comes from this building when I open the door is enough to make me gag. Your stomach may be stronger than mine, but I thought you needed a warning."

With that warning issued, she turned the key, pushed the door, and stepped back.

The men reacted in a way that would have amused Jacqui in other circumstances. The men all stepped back. Sam, the Main Roads engineer, turned green and bolted down the steps of the building to find a place to vomit. The shadow health minister, Greg, and Terry, the financial advisor, turned white and gagged as they moved further from the doorway. Tony appeared rooted to the floor. His face was white, and he looked faint, but the horror of the noxious odour transfixed him. Jacqui slammed the door, and the action jolted the minister into action.

"My God, what is that?" he asked.

"I don't know; I can't bring myself to enter the building to check. The other problem is that the building's floor serves as an undercover eating area for the kids. The smell is coming through the floorboards, so the kids won't be able to eat in the shade," Jacqui said.

When the men had pulled themselves together, Jacqui suggested a drive to Brett's place to freshen up and eat lunch. Tony travelled in Brett's ute with her, and the other men followed in their sedan. The Minister questioned her about her teaching history and the circumstances of her transfer. He asked about teacher accommodation, and Jacqui told him of her troubles at the pub and Brett's welcome offer.

Brett was a genial host and could hold his own in the conversation at the table. Greg was from a farming family and could understand the trials that Brett was experiencing. The other men were city-bred. They found the conversation both amusing and informative, but eventually, the discussion returned to the problem at hand.

After they finished lunch, Terry said, "Jacqui, why don't we go into your office? Together, we might work out the budget details for the school."

While Jacqui and Terry were busy, Brett offered to show the other men around the farm. They headed out to the ute for a tour of the property. After the first hour, it was apparent to both Jacqui and Terry that the school lacked a budget. The only available funds were those covering electricity and miscellaneous items.

"How can this kind of fiasco go unnoticed?" Jacqui asked Terry.

"I'm not sure, to be honest. It appears as though the government doesn't know the school exists."

"Well, they know enough to send me here," she replied wryly.

Over afternoon tea, Terry explained the budget to the others. Before they left, Tony said, "You are right; the repairs at the school are critical. While I can't fix things, the photos we took are enough to pressure the government. I will release the information to the media if we don't get any positive responses. You'll have protection under the Whistleblower Act, so the Department can't transfer you to the Gulf country. This problem could be ugly once the media gets involved, so maybe the government might come to the party. We'll see how we go," Tony said.

The contingent left soon after, but not before Jacqui heard Sam mutter about putting pressure on his counterpart to fix the dreadful road they had to tackle again. Jacqui felt more optimistic about the school's repairs when the ministers departed. Brett was a great host today, and his understanding and support made her realise how lucky she was to have met him on the first night in town. Without him, she would struggle to keep her head above water.

Brett breezed through the kitchen on his way to the shower before dinner. When he returned, Jacqui said, "What was the problem with the tyre on my car? Was there a nail?"

He looked up from the table and shrugged. "I can't work out what happened. There was no puncture, but the valve was loose. I tightened it, inflated the tyre, and put it in the boot as the spare. Before you go tomorrow, it might be wise to check to see that it's still inflated."

# Chapter Twelve

Jacqui received an email from the Education Minister two days after the shadow cabinet visit. The message asked Jacqui to phone his office. Hopeful that the shadow ministers had secured an agreement to refurbish the school, she rang the office. This time, the snooty receptionist connected her straight away.

"Hi, my name is Jacqui Stuart. I received an e-mail asking me to contact you."

"Yes, yes, I requested you to call me. I'm not thrilled with your tactics. Being blindsided by the opposition in parliament is not fun. If you had contacted me or informed me of the school's dire condition, we may have found funds to rectify a few problems. No matter how much fuss the opposition makes, we will not be doing any renovations this financial year."

"Minister, with all due respect, what you said is rubbish. I kept copies of the e-mail and attachment I sent you, the registered letter, the hard copies of the photos, and your written response. As you suffer from amnesia, I will remind you that I spoke to you on the phone."

"Miss Stuart, you will not back me into a corner or force me to divert funds."

"Minister, I won't even try to back you into a corner, but someone must deal with the appalling conditions at the school. Good day to you, sir."

Jacqui was furious, but working on the expression "Don't get angry, get even", she called Tony to inform him of the latest development.

While working at her desk late that afternoon, an e-mail icon appeared at the bottom of the computer screen. Tony had sent a message.

*I released the information to the media. Don't put yourself in the firing line; use 'no comment' to the questions—refer questions to either Greg or me for a statement.*

A noise in the kitchen warned Jacqui of Brett's presence. She called out,

"Come and see the e-mail Tony sent."

"Well, the show is underway," said Brett after reading the e-mail.

The next day, the small township was crawling with television crews and several newspaper photographers taking pictures of the school grounds. Journalists were speaking with residents, asking for their comments. Some photographers, unable to enter government property without proper permission, were using zoom lenses to get photos of the inside of the buildings. Jacqui debated whether to go to school as planned or go home. Instead of journalists and photographers crawling over the farm, she met them at the school gates.

"Jacqui, can you give us a statement about the repairs at the school?"

Many reporters surrounded her, yelling questions. She took Tony's warning to heart, smiled, and said, "No comment." As she waded through the crowd, they kept yelling more questions at her. As she gained the safety of the schoolyard, she turned to the reporters. "You know how it goes. I can't make any statements or comments, but I'm sure he will answer all your queries if you direct your questions to the shadow Education Minister."

Jacqui wanted to assess the students' workbooks to determine the tuition level for each class. She searched through the students' desks and found hardly any work. What on earth had this group of kids learnt? She wondered. They didn't benefit from computers, and there was no formal bookwork in evidence either. As she walked through the building, she realised that the cameras with zoom lenses could see into the room, and the pictures would make the paper's front pages. Frustrated, she grabbed the samples of work she had collected and walked to the door. She thought that one of the first things this building needed was blackout curtains.

Jacqui drove towards the safety of the farm, keeping a careful watch to ensure the media didn't follow. As she crossed the grid at the entrance, she saw Brett in one of the nearby paddocks, and he waved at her. With sudden insight, she wheeled the car around and parked at the gate. Brett walked toward her with a query on his face.

"Is there a padlock and chain for the front gate?"

"Yes, it's in the shed. I use it if I'm on holiday, but that hasn't happened in a long time. Why do we need to lock the gate?"

"Town is crawling with reporters. Sam's press release has had spectacular results, but since I didn't provide them with a statement, I imagine someone will come out looking for an exclusive. If we lock the gate, they can't get in," said Jacqui.

Brett jumped onto the four-wheeler, and Jacqui climbed into the car. Once they reached the homestead, Brett walked around the building to the shed at the back. Jacqui thought the shed always looked like a shambles, but Brett still found what he wanted. He walked towards the large bench at the back of the shed, where he pulled out the padlock and chain from a pile of metal.

"Do you want to ride back with me?"

"I might as well. I'll make sure you do it right," said Jacqui.

She climbed onto the back of the bike, glad she was wearing jeans. As soon as she seated herself, Brett took off, and she grabbed him around the waist to prevent herself from falling. Once they reached the gate, he wrapped the chain around the gate and the post twice, then secured it with the padlock.

"There are two keys to the house. Put them on your key ring for a few days until the storm dies," said Brett.

That night's news led with the story of "The Bush kids the government forgot." The school videos were dismal to watch, and the lens was powerful enough to see inside the classroom. Still shots of the toilets, the school grounds, and the old building added to the overall effect of total neglect.

A journalist interviewed Sam, and he clarified that Jacqui had contacted all the local authorities. The Minister described the school's shocking conditions and the lack of technology, which prevented her from teaching the national curriculum. He spoke of the unsanitary state of the toilets and the workplace health and safety breaches in the classroom and on the school grounds. The newscast finished when the reporter announced that the Minister of Education was unavailable for comment.

The government's embarrassment continued the next day, when both state and national newspapers took up the story. Journalists pressured the Education Minister for comment, then diverted their attention to the Premier. The press asked questions at every meeting and badgered him for a response. Tony and Greg made the most of the situation, placing themselves in the public eye. Tony emailed Jacqui to let her know they intended to keep the pressure on until the Premier conceded.

# Chapter Thirteen

The grounds teemed with workers. The school closed when the local council health inspector slapped a ban on the toilets. The ban embarrassed the government, which folded ungraciously. The school was undergoing refurbishment and an upgrade. After fumigating the old building, the builders stripped it to the frame. They constructed shelves in the old room, providing the pupils with another space to use.

Jacqui buzzed with excitement, pleased that she had achieved something when her predecessor failed. She hadn't met her charges yet, but felt sure their response to the improvements would be positive. Although unable to access the site while work was underway, Jacqui drove in daily to view the changes. She could not enter the site, so most of her observations were from the fence line. Most of the workers acknowledged Jacqui, recognising that she was the reason for their recent hefty paychecks.

After completing her daily check on the repairs' progress, Jacqui drove home. As she neared the gates, stock milling in the front paddock appeared. She had never seen the stock in that place and wondered why Brett had turned the cattle out there. Although he had a yard around the house with livestock in the outer area, they also had access to the hay shed. She unlocked the gate and pushed it open, hoping the animals didn't rush her.

She drove along the driveway and towards the shed, which had a padlock secured on it. Brett's ute was missing, and he hadn't taken the dogs. The gate to the nearest paddock stood open, and the cattle walked around in the yard. Jacqui looked for Brett, assuming he must be nearby. She scanned the area, but there was no sign of him. She untied the dogs and sent them to round up the cattle. They needed a few instructions, particularly Molly, because the unexpected muster excited her. Jacqui patted both dogs and handed them a treat when she locked up the stock.

A short time later, she heard the ute. When Brett walked into the kitchen, he said, "What happened in the yard? Manure is near the shed, and the hay looks like elephants have attacked it."

Jacqui shrugged. "When I got home, the cattle from the top paddock roamed in the driveway. The gate was open, so I used the dogs to muster the stock and push them back. I didn't think you'd let the cattle out on purpose. If I did the wrong thing, I'm sorry."

"That's strange. I didn't let the cattle out. They can do too much damage in that yard. Thanks for putting them back."

When the workers finished repairing the school, Jacqui returned to work. She still helped Brett in the morning, and they had an established routine. On her first day with students, she had a flat tyre on her small SUV.

"This is getting to be trying. Should we report this to the police? I know they cannot act, but at least it will be on the record."

"Yeah, it won't hurt. You eat while I change the tyre so that you won't be late on your first day with the kids."

That morning, it took a while to settle everyone. The kids chattered and ran around, looking at the changes. Usually, most students arrive at the school by bus, but today, they came by car. The parents wanted to meet Jacqui and tour the school buildings' improvements.

One dad, a farmer with a slasher, came into town the day before and cut the yard's grass. There were no picturesque gardens, but the improvements to the school made her smile. While it looked rough, at least the kids could now play outside, and if snakes lurked around, they could see them.

The twenty-five students kept Jacqui busy. When two mums offered to help, Jacqui grabbed the offer with both hands and together, the three of them worked out a roster. She rotated the students through different activities; each student worked with her and the mums daily.

Her helpers didn't come in on Mondays and Fridays, but Jacqui roped in one dad to help with sports on Fridays. She found the work stimulating and parental help invaluable. The idea of running an open day took hold. She wanted to invite the people interested in viewing the improvements and those who instigated the changes. Should she contact the workers and ask them to come?

The cars lined the entire length of the street outside the school. Many of the visitors were locals who wanted to see the school updates. The media furore in town also sparked interest. She observed a white sedan pull up at the curb as the guests walked around. When the doors opened, and four men in business suits stepped out, her face split into a huge grin. She abandoned a group of parents and rushed over to greet the newcomers.

"Hello! Thank you for coming. You all deserve a hug. I'm so happy you came; I'll pretend not to notice if you want to campaign," Jacqui said.

After shaking hands all around, she led Sam, Tony, Greg and Terry into the midst of the parents. Once she introduced the Ministers, people drifted over to speak to them. During the afternoon, a few tradies who worked there came for a quick look. Peter, the supervisor on the refurbishment project, took the time to visit. As the afternoon wound up, Peter cornered Jacqui and said,

"I'll be working in the district for a while. Do you want to have a meal? There are no strings, just two friends getting together. What do you think?"

Taken by surprise, Jacqui said, "Can I take a rain check on that?"

"Sure, I'll give you my number. I'll be around for another four weeks."

As she locked up the school, Jacqui sighed. The open day was a tremendous success, and although a few of the repairs were temporary fixes, the school was far more pleasant than before the changes. With everything good in her world, Jacqui headed for her car. She couldn't wait to tell Brett of the day's success. The breath caught in Jacqui's throat, and she slapped her hand over her mouth when she saw her car. She shook her head, denying the evidence before her. The driver's side door and panels of her vehicle had sustained significant paintwork scratches. It appeared someone had run a key or a coin across the paintwork. She raced to the passenger side of the car; scratches marred that side, too. Fists clenched, and teeth gritted, Jacqui surveyed this senseless act of vandalism. The culprit must be a local, but she didn't understand who it could be. Who was angry enough to target her? Sure, she pushed a few people to get the school fixed, but she couldn't imagine peeved-off government Ministers skulking around with the sole aim of disfiguring her car.

"Well, this takes the shine off the day," she thought.

Resigned to the expense of repairs, Jacqui drove toward home. Her eyes widened as she turned onto the road leading to the farm. There were animals out; as Jacqui came closer, she realised they were cattle. She recognised the stock and knew the herd milling around on the road belonged to Brett. Slowing the car, she crawled beside the paddock, and sure enough, she came to a break in the fence. This gap was not a natural break, as the cut in the wire created a significant gateway for the cattle.

Jacqui pulled out her phone and dialled Brett's number.

"Brett, the cattle are on the road; you must get here quickly. I'll wait for you."

A string of profanities spewed from the phone before he said,

"I'm on my way."

Jacqui didn't know what to do as she waited. Would the cattle move away from the car if she drove behind them? When she did a U-turn, she returned to where a group of stragglers grazed by the side of the road. She beeped the horn, and the cattle lifted their heads. Another beep, and the stock turned around and trotted towards the gap in the fence. She followed behind them in the car, hoping Brett and the dogs would arrive soon.

The noise of the four-wheeler coming made her sigh with relief. She watched as Brett dispatched the dogs to push the stock towards the fence breach. Jacqui parked at the other end to prevent the cattle from straying too far. Brett left her with the dogs and raced back to the shed when the herd was back in the paddock. When he returned, he had wire and fence strainers, and he set to work fixing the fence with grim determination.

"Is there something I can do?"

"Yeah, pour me a large drink. When I finish this, we need to talk."

"Okay. Do you want me to take the dogs with me?"

"Take Barney; Molly can stay with me. I won't be long," he said.

Jacqui called the old dog and lifted him into the vehicle. As Brett turned to say something, he caught sight of the side of her car.

"You're kidding me, right?"

"Afraid not."

As she drove back to the house, she thought of the mishaps that had occurred since she moved in with Brett. The problems didn't begin immediately, but once they started, they happened with monotonous regularity. The earlier damage had a nuisance value, but the situation escalated with vandalism to her car and cattle on the road. Someone in the town disliked her, and it also appeared that they had a grudge against Brett, too.

The noise of the ute outside and the slam of the door reminded her to get Brett a stiff drink. She laughed to herself. She knew there was no alcohol in the house, so the drink had to be coffee.

Brett walked into the kitchen, threw his hat on the table, and said, "Talk to me."

She guessed he wanted to find out what had happened to her SUV. She shrugged her shoulders.

"There's not much to tell. We had a terrific day, with people everywhere. When I locked up to go home, I saw the damage. It's on both sides of the car. I didn't notice anyone hanging around the vehicles, but then I was busy with parents, politicians and tradies. The repairs will cost a fortune. I'm not sure whether to scream or cry."

"After you left this morning, I rang Trent, but there's not much he can do. I'll tell him what's happened tonight; at least it's logged," said Brett. "I'm worried; these episodes are getting worse than nuisance value. The damage to your car is serious. If you hadn't been the first person to happen upon the stock, their presence on the road might have had grave consequences."

"Have you thought of asking the guy next door if he's had any trouble? He might have seen an unfamiliar car around because whoever is doing this needs transport unless they live across the road".

"I'll give Jack a ring now; ask if he knows anything."

Brett's phone call revealed that Jack had seen a station wagon parked in their gateway a few days before. He couldn't tell the model but said it was an old, brown vehicle. Brett asked him to pass that news on to the police, hoping someone else saw the car.

# Chapter Fourteen

Brett found working with the dogs relieved much of the pressure he had previously felt as he moved around the property. He was no longer alone all day, and even though the dogs didn't understand, he held conversations with them as he worked. Barney looked as though he was considering everything Brett said. Brett had to laugh at his dog when he head tilted to one side as though weighing up the possibilities.

Why had he never thought of using working dogs? Things could have been easier for his mum and him if they had had dogs to help. God bless Jacqui; she had changed his life in so many ways. He was sure that his mum would have liked her. What do I do when the time comes for her to leave? He wondered. She had become such a big part of life on the farm; he didn't want to imagine her not being here.

Against his better judgment, Brett found himself disturbingly drawn to Jacqui. The belief that 'if it's too good to be true, it probably is' had been brought home to him when dealing with Aunt Gloria. Should he guard his heart now, or was Jacqui the exception to the rule? As Brett ran his hands through his hair, he sighed. He wished he had someone to confide in, to help sort out the jumble of emotions that had come to the fore with Jacqui's presence in his life.

How long did she intend to stay? Long enough to turn his world upside down and leave him gutted when she left? He shook himself to get his thoughts away from that depressing scenario. He focused on an idea that had been on his mind for the last few days. Why not ring Sid and tell him how well this was going? Should he ask Sid to pay a visit? He could check that Brett wasn't teaching the dogs, particularly Molly, any bad habits.

That night, he asked Jacqui, "Are you okay with inviting Sid for a few days?"

"That sounds good. See if he can stay for the weekend to give you on-site instruction. I must ensure he doesn't catch me playing with the dogs, or he might scold me."

Brett laughed. "I think he might guess you spoil them."

Two nights later, Jacqui pulled up to the shed and, as she got out of the car, heard another vehicle approaching. She smiled as she recognised the ute. After his conversation with Brett, Sid accepted the invitation to join them for the weekend, but he needed to bring a dog. He had only one rescue dog in his care, so bringing it along shouldn't be a problem.

Sid came toward her and hugged her. The two strolled towards Sid's vehicle, and Jacqui saw his latest rescue. The dog in the crate cowered when it saw her. Its tattered brown coat was dirty, and huge sores covered its body. Jacqui made a distressed sound; Sid put his arm around her. "Can you see why I didn't leave her for someone else to feed?"

"Were our dogs in this condition when you got them?"

"No, I have got to most dogs before they reach this stage. People told me the owner beat the dog, but I couldn't convince the guy to sell her. He kept saying she needed a firm hand, which meant he hit her. I threatened him with the RSPCA, and he folded. He was trying to get rid of her while saving face. He would have killed her if I hadn't got to her when I did."

Jacqui turned to reply when Brett called from inside the house,

"Are you two coming inside, or will you spend the night talking?"

Sid undid the cage and coaxed the reluctant dog out. He walked to the veranda with the dog on his heels and instructed it to lie in the corner. With his hand outstretched, he reached for Brett and shook his hand.

"Sorry mate, you can't begrudge an old man spending time with a beautiful girl?"

"Don't get any ideas, mate. I saw her first," Brett said with a laugh.

"Okay, now you two have finished being macho, we might have a cuppa and settle Sid into the spare room."

Over dinner that night, Brett said, "We've had problems with vandalism and interference with the stock. Jacqui's car has taken the brunt of vandalism, two flat tyres, and damage from someone keying it. Someone has let the stock out of their paddock twice, and the third time they walked through a cut in the fence, Jacqui found them on the road."

Sid voiced the concern that had been nagging at Brett from the start. "You realise it has to be someone who has made friends with the dogs? Otherwise, they would bark if a stranger were walking about."

"That was my fear," Brett said.

"Oh, my God! That's even worse. So, the dogs recognise this person and make no fuss while they roam around causing damage," Jacqui said.

"Why don't we leave it until tomorrow? We can look at putting up sensor lights and security cameras in the shed," suggested Brett.

With the problem shelved for a brief moment, the conversation turned to current affairs. The three friends discussed everything from Sid's work to the federal government. Sid insisted on washing the dishes, and Jacqui grabbed the tea towel to dry.

Suddenly, there was a commotion outdoors. Sid's dog, Shelia, chained up at the shed with the other two dogs, was making a fuss, barking and growling. Brett grabbed a torch and headed for the door. "I'll go".

Sid wiped his hands on the small towel hung over the cooker's rail and walked to the door. Just as he opened the door, all the dogs began howling wildly. Barking and snarling, they hurled themselves against the end of their chains.

"Damnation! Jac, call the police," Sid said and raced outside. Jacqui dialled the number with trembling hands. In a shaky voice, she told Trent, the police officer, what she knew, and he assured her he was on his way.

Jacqui raced to the veranda and peered out. A person was rushing towards her, and she realised it was Sid when he was closer.

"Get a wet cloth and ice. Brett is unconscious. I'll ring the ambulance while you get the stuff," Sid said.

They hurried back to the shed with the first aid supplies in hand. Brett lay stretched out on his side; evidently, Sid had moved him into the recovery position. Jacqui let out a cry and raced to where the inert figure lay.

"Calm yourself, sweetheart. He's taken a blow to the head. The best we can do for now is to apply the ice pack. If you wipe his face with the cloth, it might help bring him around."

Jacqui wiped Brett's forehead, cheeks, and mouth while tears ran down her face. His stillness troubled her; she heard stories of people with head injuries, and the resulting brain damage that sometimes occurred caused the victim to die. The siren wailed in the night. The lone police officer in Manwarring was on his way. Jacqui prayed the ambulance was close.

"Jac, meet him in the driveway," Sid said. "Otherwise, he'll go to the house."

Jacqui scrunched up the cloth and raced out to meet the police vehicle.

As Trent viewed the scene and checked Brett, the ambulance sirens shattered the nighttime stillness. Jacqui ran to meet the emergency vehicle and directed them to the shed. The paramedics loaded Brett into the ambulance, but Jacqui and Sid were unable to accompany him because Trent needed them to give a statement. They recounted their story, each filling in gaps if the other paused.

Trent said, "When Brett told me what happened today, I knew the behaviour was escalating, and that was worrying. We'll get technicians here to check the scene, but I'm not hopeful of finding much."

Trent left, and Jacqui and Sid were preparing to follow the ambulance when the phone rang. Jacqui considered not answering it, but changed her mind.

"Hi, sweetie, how's the country?" her dad said.

"Dad, I can't talk now. Someone attacked Brett, and Sid and I were getting ready to drive to Lonsdale to the hospital. I'll catch you later."

Upon arrival, they found paperwork that needed to be completed before anyone could provide an update. The doctor sought them out.

"Your friend is still unconscious. We are carrying out scans to determine the level of damage to his skull. At the moment, I can't tell you anymore."

Hours later, with nerves stretched to their limit, Jacqui watched a man walk to the waiting room's door. She looked again at the stranger listlessly and then jumped to her feet.

"Dad!"

"How is he?" he asked.

Jacqui burst into tears, and Colin Stuart hugged his daughter. She told him the little they knew of Brett's condition when the tears dried.

"You must be Sid," Colin said. The two men shook hands, and Colin sat beside Sid. He patted the chair and said, "Sit here, Jac. It might be a long night."

She sniffed back tears as she told Colin of the vandalism and the harassment that had occurred since her arrival.

"Sid's dog set off the alarm because the police believe whoever is doing this has befriended our dogs. We think it was when Brett got hit that our dogs went crazy."

The night was edging towards morning when a tired-looking doctor emerged.

"Who's the next of kin here?"

"Brett has no next of kin. I'm a close friend, so please update me," Jacqui said.

"Okay, your boyfriend is conscious and coherent, so you can visit him individually. We'll keep him for a day or two because I want to check on the concussion. He's had a nasty blow to the head, and I suspect he will have some side effects. The police said they would wait until the next day to talk to him. I'll catch up with you later today to decide how many days he needs to stay." The doctor rubbed his temples and then disappeared into the rooms behind the swing door.

Jacqui breathed a sigh of relief. "Is it okay, Sid, if I go first?"

When Jacqui walked away, Colin said to Sid,

"Tell me about Jacqui and Brett. Is there more between those two than a border and a landlord?"

"Yeah, I'm sure there is, although neither has acted on it yet. They make a great team, and I'm sure they would be good together."

Colin just nodded.

# Chapter Fifteen

B rett returned home three days after the attack. He was still suffering from dizzy spells, and a constant headache made him irritable. Sid returned home for a few days, and Colin stayed in town to help during the day while Jacqui was at work.

Jacqui saw a different side of her father. He assisted with stock feeding and other farm jobs that Brett couldn't do. While not a country person, he tackled the tasks with enthusiasm and good humour.

Brett spent much of the day resting in the lounge room. Having been fit and healthy for most of his life, he was a grumpy patient. Even in bed, the dizziness was debilitating.

Jacqui checked on him in the morning before work and spent as much time as possible after school. She was sure the healthy version of Brett was more pleasant than the patient. His foul temper and constant whining were not sides of him that had ever surfaced.

Colin watched his daughter become less patient and more upset by Brett's rudeness. Sympathy for her plight forced him to speak.

"I understand Brett's hard to cope with, but be patient. It must frustrate him to see himself transformed from a healthy man to an invalid. He'll come right; give it time."

Four days later, Colin drove Brett back to the hospital to have the stitches removed. He was returning home, and Sid intended to collect Brett from the hospital and return to the farm. With his affairs in order, Sid proposed staying for another week or two until Brett felt better.

Brett hoped by now the dizziness would have receded. Sometimes there was no dizziness, and at other times he had to sit quickly to avoid falling. He watched Jacqui wilt and knew that he was at fault. She tried to put on a cheerful face, but the smile never reached her eyes. Even though he knew his behaviour was unreasonable, he couldn't stop himself. He admonished himself and promised to behave better, but then she said something, and his helplessness boiled over; he yelled at her.

With too much idle time, he fretted about his relationship with Jacqui. To his mind, she showed him only the same warm affection she showed both Sid and her father. With nothing to do but worry, he convinced himself that she would up and leave, breaking his heart.

He cursed himself for being a fool. How had he let Jacqui mean so much to him? It might be better to push her into moving out before he was so in love with her that he couldn't function in her absence.

Sid watched with concern as Brett badgered and bullied Jacqui. He led her to believe he needed to check everything she did, pushing away any help she offered. One night, when Brett had complained of a headache and retired, Jacqui said,

"I'm sure he blames me. I'm not sure why I'm at fault or what I did to cause all this trouble. If I'm the problem, I should find somewhere else to stay. What do you think?"

Before Sid answered her, the door flew open. The scowl on Brett's face shrivelled her heart. It was unclear how much of the conversation he had overheard, but what he had heard had made him furious.

"You don't have to stay here fussing and carrying on. Why not leave and save us both the trouble of living in the same house?"

"Son, you're a bloody idiot. You're rude, and Jacqui only wants to help. The attack was not her fault. I should leave so things can go back to normal."

"Don't stay on my account," Brett spat out.

Jacqui looked at Sid as Brett walked out. Sid sighed and rose from his seat.

"I'll talk to him to see if I can work out what's happening in that muddled brain."

Sid tapped on the door. There was no response. He pushed the door open, walked to the chair beside the bed, and sat.

"What do you want?" Brett snapped.

"Mate, we want the kind, honourable farmer we both met to return. We're tired of the grouch, sick of hearing you criticise and find fault. I understand that this injury and the dizziness are debilitating, but that doesn't give you the right to hurt the people who care for you," Sid said.

Brett ran his hands through his hair and shrugged.

"I heard Jacqui say she is considering moving. God, I guess the idea of her leaving just unhinged me. How do I stop caring for her? She will go at the end of the transfer period, and I don't know how I'll manage without her."

"Have you told her that ?"

"No, what if she doesn't care for me, and it becomes too awkward? She would move out in a heartbeat if she thought I wanted her."

"Mate, you underestimate her. Apologise and sort this out."

Brett nodded. "I owe you an apology, too. I'm sorry for being such a grouch."

"Apology accepted, but now fix this thing with Jacqui. If you don't sort this out, you won't have to wait for the Department to transfer her; she'll pack up and leave herself."

That afternoon, Jacqui put off going home for as long as possible. Not wanting to go home was ridiculous, but she had grown tired of the criticism and nitpicking. Aside from her work, her only interaction was with Brett; lately, there had been no joy in that.

On the drive home, she remembered Peter's invitation. She had no romantic interest in him, but the thought of a night out made her smile. Over dinner that night, she broached the matter of her meal with Peter.

"I'm not your keeper. You need to make up your mind."

He looked angry at her suggestion, so Jacqui didn't push the issue. Dinner resumed, and Brett did the dishes before heading to his office when they finished.

"Will you be much longer? That show you wanted to see starts in ten minutes."

"Can you stick a disc in and record it?" he asked.

He spent the rest of the night in his office and was still there when Jacqui went to bed. When she said goodnight, he mumbled something and returned to the computer in front of him.

That night, she mulled over Brett's response to Peter's invitation as she lay in bed. Before his poor behaviour, she preferred to go for dinner with Brett. Perhaps I should suggest that, but he had made no advances and shown no interest in her beyond the border; he didn't even want her as a border. Confused and angry at Brett's behaviour, she accepted the invitation.

Jacqui helped with the evening jobs on Friday night and then prepared for her dinner date. She agreed to meet at the Palace restaurant in Lonsdale. Brett sat in the lounge room watching TV, and she walked in to say goodbye. He eyed her over and raised an eyebrow.

"What? Do I look overdressed or something?"

"No, I'm sure your date will appreciate that outfit."

She felt uncomfortable, as though she was wearing something daring and provocative.

"Thanks. That's how to give a girl confidence, and it is not a date." She stalked out of the room. I am not changing this dress just because he is a prude, she said to herself.

While still unhappy to drive on the road from Manwarring to Lonsdale, Jacqui conceded that the road repairs significantly improved what was little better than a cattle track before the repairs. In the future, the council will divert traffic and resurface this road. It was good news all around.

She made decent time and pulled up a few minutes early at the Palace. The valet took the car keys and disappeared with her vehicle. She entered the restaurant, and a friendly server greeted her, directing her to a table. She pretended to read the menu for the first ten minutes, glancing at her wristwatch periodically. The server returned and asked her if she wanted a drink while she waited; Jacqui accepted and sat nursing her drink for the next few minutes. Peter was now twenty minutes late. When she signalled the server to ask if any messages were left for her, he replied, "No". Glancing at the time again, she would wait ten more minutes and then go.

As she rose from the table, intending to leave, Peter strolled into the restaurant. He was in no hurry, and she knew he had been drinking when he spoke.

"In a rush to see me, were you?"

"I was leaving. You're half an hour late. I thought you'd stand me up." Jacqui's eyes narrowed, and she vibrated with anger.

"Time got away; you know how it is?"

Jacqui gritted her teeth and vowed to make the most of it now he had arrived. She was angry that he hadn't apologised for his tardiness, as though she didn't count. The meal was expensive, but it was worth every penny. Peter was pleasant company, but Jacqui became concerned about the quantity of alcohol he consumed. He kept pressuring her to have more, but she declined as she had to drive home.

As the meal progressed, Peter slipped in the odd, suggestive comment, and Jacqui felt uncomfortable. She excused herself to go to the ladies' room and, once inside, stood looking in the mirror. How could she get out of this without turning the evening sour? He commented about her "showing her appreciation" for the meal and the night out. There is no way I'm going there, Jacqui decided. She left the toilets with a loud sigh and returned to the table. There seemed to be a problem; Peter was arguing with the server.

"What is the problem?"

"This bloody wowser won't serve any more alcohol. I've had enough, according to this bloke."

Jacqui sighed with relief. Amen to that. "Could we finish with coffee?" she said to the server with a hopeful smile.

"I don't want frigging coffee; I want another beer," he shouted.

Jacqui moved away from the table and signalled the receptionist. "Can I have the bill? I'll try to move him after I pay." The woman tallied the cost, and Jacqui paid with her credit card. Peter stood and shouted at the beleaguered server, and as she moved toward the table, the security guard entered the room.

"You have to leave, mate," said the burly bouncer. The bouncer grabbed an arm and frog-marched him from the restaurant when he resisted. Jacqui flushed with embarrassment and ducked her head. She followed the two men out of the restaurant and signalled the valet to collect her car. She hoped there were no parents from the school at the restaurant that night.

Once he got outside, Peter decided Jacqui should show her appreciation. As the valet pulled up in her car, he grabbed her arm and pulled her towards him. She gagged; he reeked of alcohol and stale sweat and pawed her with clumsy fingers. As she tried to wriggle out of his grasp, his fingers closed over her arm more tightly. He moved his face close to her, intending to kiss her. He raised his hand to slap her, but a hand came out and grabbed his arm, preventing the slap. Jacqui dug the heel of her shoe into his foot, and he yelped and let her go.

"That's enough, mate," said the valet. "The lady isn't interested, and you need to go home and sober up. I'll order a cab for you, and you can come by tomorrow and collect your car."

Jacqui used the distraction to walk to her car. Peter continued to shout at the valet, insisting that he could drive and demanding the keys to his vehicle. Jacqui drove away. Her reprieve from the unpleasant night overshadowed her guilt at leaving the valet to deal with the spectacle of a drunk patron.

# Chapter Sixteen

When the alarm sounded the next morning, Brett rolled over and groaned. He stayed awake half the night, waiting for Jacqui to come home. Either he fell asleep, or she returned in the early morning because he had no memory of her arrival.

He had put off talking to her and apologising for his behaviour, so she took refuge in another man's company. He was a fool; everything he thought he had sorted out about his feelings for Jacqui was too late. The joy of having her in the house dimmed as he understood the one reason she might stay out so late. He ripped off the covers and grabbed his work clothes. He stalked towards the kitchen and glanced back toward Jacqui's bedroom. The door to her room remained closed, showing she was inside and likely still asleep. Last night, he turned off her alarm before retiring, thinking she might appreciate a sleep-in if she returned late. Now, faced with the empty kitchen and the arduous task of feeding the cattle alone, he was angry at himself for trying to make up for his spiteful display last night.

After a quick breakfast, Brett made sandwiches to hold him over until dinnertime. If Brett took the dogs, he could muster the cattle that strayed into the next-door property, and he needn't face Jacqui until he returned for dinner. That ought to fix her! Maybe he should go out tonight, have dinner, and see if he could pick up some company for the evening.

He cursed Jacqui's fickle nature as he struggled with the hay bales and the endless procession of gates. He might have hit on her if he thought she'd pay out after a meal. He must be going mad; he had lived with her for the last three months and would bet his reputation on her integrity. What was he thinking?

When Jacqui left, he would once again be alone. Why couldn't he interest the only person he had wanted in his life? What did Peter have that captured Jacqui's interest? He had convinced himself that she had no interest in money; was it his physique or personality that attracted Jacqui? Brett had never met the guy, so comparing himself to an unknown adversary proved pointless. He tried to shake off images of Jacqui with another guy, but wasn't having much luck.

Slumped under a tree with the dogs lolling on the surrounding ground, he ate the unappetizing sandwiches for lunch. Once he got the energy, he'd send the dogs out to round up the stock, strolling through the loose wire into the neighbouring property. When one post fell, the wire in that section of the fence let go, giving the cattle free access to whatever feed was on the adjoining property.

The phone he'd left in the ute rang. Rousing himself, he picked up his mobile and checked the caller ID; it was Jacqui. He knew he couldn't speak to her without losing his temper; better to ignore her than shout at her. He clicked the phone off, retrieved the fencing gear and called the dogs.

The job took him twice as long as expected. The cattle didn't cooperate, and the dogs worked overtime to collect them into a mob Brett could push back over the fence line. With the stock herded away, he moved the ute to block their path and set to repairing the post and wire. Jacki rang twice more, and each time, she left a message. He felt angry at her concern; he knew she worried about his safety, but his anger at her still burned too brightly for him to speak to her calmly. Finally, his guilt took effect, and the next time the phone rang, Brett answered it.

"Brett, where are you? I've been frantic with worry."

At the genuine anxiety in her voice, he bristled. After abandoning him last night, she didn't sound concerned now.

"Settle down. I don't need a babysitter, and I don't need a thousand messages on my phone. I'll be there soon."

Once he had confined the cattle to his property, Brett collected his tools and lifted Barney into the ute. Molly leapt up beside her mate, and Brett turned the vehicle towards home. He hoped he could keep his temper when speaking to Jacqui. As much as Brett wanted to resolve their problem, he feared that her presence would only make it worse. How would he control his temper when she was present if he couldn't hold his anger in check while he sat in the middle of a paddock?

When Jacqui woke after her night out, she experienced a moment of bewilderment. It appeared to be late. The sunlight filtered through the window, and the bird sounds of early morning were absent. She stretched and climbed out of bed. The readout on the clock read nine o'clock. Did she forget to set the alarm, or had it gone off, and she'd slept through the noise? By now, Brett must have fed the cattle without her.

Last night, after the debacle of the meal, sleep couldn't come soon enough. Walking to the bathroom, the smell of cigarette smoke clung to her hair and clothes. A long shower would be ideal, but mindful of the water shortage, she kept it brief. Once clean and smoke-free, she pulled out a pair of jeans and a T-shirt.

Brett was not in the kitchen, although the breakfast dishes in the sink confirmed he had eaten earlier. Jacqui made slices of toast, poured a cup of tea, and then walked outside to see where Brett was. His ute and the dogs were both missing. Usually, he left her a note if he went out into the paddocks. She scanned the kitchen but did not find a letter; the only way to reach him was to ring his mobile. The phone went to voicemail. Either he had it turned off, or it was out of range.

Seated at her desk in the little room she used as an office, Jacqui listened for the sound of the ute. Lunchtime arrived, and she made a large plate of sandwiches, waiting for him, expecting his return. An hour later, she ate lunch and left the remaining sandwiches wrapped in plastic in the fridge.

As the day wore on, Jacqui's worry increased and repeated tries to contact him failed. With a worried frown, she walked outside and scanned the skyline. There was no sign of Brett. Jacqui fed the chooks and penned them for the night. She mixed up the feed in the shed for the half a dozen poddy calves living in the side paddock. Once Jacqui tipped the contents of the buckets into the feeders, she put out the dogs' feed, expecting their imminent arrival. Moving the cattle from the silage paddock might be difficult without the dogs, but she hoped they would cooperate as this move occurred daily.

The sun started its descent, and darkness approached as she returned to the house. What to do? Did she call out neighbours to help search or sit and wait? Fear crawled along her spine, and dread assailed her. He had been missing all day; perhaps she should have called for help a long time ago. She gave the phone one more try. This time, he answered the phone.

"Brett, where are you? I've been frantic with worry."

"Settle down. I don't need a babysitter, and I don't need a thousand messages on my phone. I'll be there soon," and with that, he hung up on her.

By the time the ute pulled up outside, her anger had peaked. She listened as he let the dogs off, followed by the slam of the wire door as he came onto the veranda.

"Relax," she told herself. Yelling when Brett entered the kitchen would be counterproductive. She clenched her fists and set her jaw in an attempt not to fly at him when he strolled into the kitchen. He looked dishevelled and dusty. His eyes had a defiant glint, and his chin tilted up stubbornly.

"Where have you been?"

"None of your damn business."

Her eyes widened, and her mouth gaped open. In all the time they had lived together, Brett had never spoken in such a brusque manner. What on earth was the problem? She took a deep breath and raked her hand through her hair in frustration. "I thought something might have happened to you."

"I'm an adult; I can look after myself. Is dinner ready, or must I go to the pub?"

Jacqui rounded on him. Her eyes glinted, and her lush lips formed a thin line. "Damn you! I'm over men who think they can treat me like dirt. If dinner were ready, I'd put poison in it for you, so you'd best take your rotten mood and get pissed with those other losers at the pub."

"Fine. Don't wait up; I might find some action." With that, he stalked out the door. The ute roared up the driveway, and with a loud screech, it slammed across the grate at the entrance.

Jacqui moved around the kitchen, preparing food she no longer wanted to eat. Her fingers trembled, and a massive ache lodged in her stomach. Last night's comment on the way she looked was mean and hurtful. During Brett's recovery, his personality changed, becoming judgmental and petty. Had the injury changed his nature permanently? The guy she had become so fond of had transformed into a monster before her eyes.

What did he mean, find some action of his own? Her concern for him clouded her brain; was this still about last night? His behaviour was so out of character that there must be a reason; tomorrow morning, she intended to find the cause of the problem. She would have to find alternative accommodation if they couldn't resolve their differences. The thought of leaving the farm brought tears to her eyes.

# Chapter Seventeen

It was pitch dark. Jacqui woke with a start. What had woken her? She heard a noise in the kitchen, and someone stumbled along the hallway. So, he had come home drunk. The ten-kilometre drive along the dirt road to his place was difficult at the best of times. Attempting the drive while inebriated was courting disaster. In her time as his boarder, she had seen Brett drink, but mindful of his obligations on the farm, he only ever drank a few. She rolled over, pulled the sheet up further, and sank into sleep.

The house was silent, so Brett hadn't woken up yet. The alarm beeped, and Jacqui reached out her hand to stop the noise. She grabbed a quick drink in the kitchen and walked to the shed. The dogs greeted her, and she stopped to pat them before collecting the ute.

Once she backed the ute into the hay shed, she offloaded the bales she would need and then drove out to the paddocks to feed the cattle. She knew Brett's route, and the stock no longer frightened her. She began throwing out the feed. The job was challenging for one person due to frequent stopping and starting, and the need to open and close gates. By the time she finished, her tummy felt hollow, but she had more jobs to complete. She let the dogs off, fed them, fed the poddy calves, and finally let the chooks out.

When Jacqui reached the house, she was hungry, tired and peeved off. Feeding animals and doing Brett's jobs was not how she wanted to spend her Sunday. He had not done any morning tasks, and he still wasn't out of bed. She drank her cup of tea as she prodded the cooking food. Jacqui muttered to herself as she threw eggs and bacon into a pan and thrust the bread into the toaster. The toast popped, and Jacqui threw the bacon and eggs onto the plate. She fumed at his behaviour as she ate the meal that should have been breakfast two hours ago.

Brett surfaced a little after lunchtime. He looked worse for wear, and his intoxication last night showed in the colour of his face and the scowl that showed a massive hangover. Jacqui made no move to talk to him and left him to his own devices. Feeling calmer, Jacqui decided to cook dinner after putting the chooks away and then tackle the problem. After collecting a drink, she returned to her office and stayed there for a large part of the afternoon.

On her way out to feed the chooks, Brett walked past her, clean-shaven and dressed in his best clothes.

"I'm going out. I don't need dinner, and I'll be late." His eyes glinted defiantly, and he raised his chin as if daring her to complain.

Jacqui ran her hands through her hair. "Please, Brett, we need to talk. I don't want to live this way."

"Well, don't; leave whenever you like. I'm not forcing you to stay."

She stamped her foot and glared at him.

"If it didn't occur to you, I'm not the farmer here. Who do you think put the cattle away last night and let them out this morning? Who do you imagine fed the bales out for the stock this morning and fed the poddy calves? I can't help it if you're chasing a hot tart. You're the farmer here and need to take that responsibility."

"You're such a whiz-bang; you do it for a while." Brett climbed into his car and drove away.

Jacqui stood watching him drive away. Her chest ached, and her stomach rolled. Tears welled in her eyes. What had just happened here? Today, he was angrier than he had been yesterday. What had upset him? If he talked to her, they could sort this out. She could pack up and leave, but knew she would miss him too much. In ordinary circumstances, he was even-tempered and thoughtful. She realised that her attraction to him had nothing to do with what he was but who he was.

After a sleepless night, Jacqui was relieved to see Brett in the kitchen making breakfast. The appearance of normality was pleasing, but the problem, whatever it was, needed to be discussed.

"Good morning."

Brett glanced at her, and something flashed in his eyes, but it disappeared before she decided what the expression meant.

"Yeah," he said.

She sat at the table and waited for the toast to pop from the toaster. Brett sat in his usual place opposite, and an awkward silence descended upon the room. Jacqui broke the silence.

"We need to talk about why you're angry. After our conversation, if you still wish for me to leave, I will. At the moment, I don't know what I've done wrong."

He glared at Jacqui, and an expression of disgust crossed his face.

"You're the talk of the town. I heard about you at the pub, and all the guys are giving me winks and nudges."

"What? I don't understand. Why am I a topic of conversation in the pub?"

"The dinner date was so much more than Peter hoped for."

Her eyebrow rose. "That's astonishing, considering how the night ended."

"What happened that night?"

"Understand that it wasn't supposed to be a date. We agreed to meet at seven o'clock in Lonsdale. He was half an hour late and didn't even apologise. He had been drinking before he arrived. His excuse for being late was people, to see, things to do."

"Sometimes people get held up," Brett said.

"Then why not leave a message? He thought he was on a sure thing. During the meal, he drank excessively and made crude comments. While I tried to work out how to leave without a fuss, the server refused to serve him more beer. Amid shouting and swearing, security evicted him, and I had to pay for the meal. He insisted I return to his place to show my gratitude for the evening. Oh, and just so you get the full picture while trying to convince me to be grateful, he abused me, and if not for the valet's intervention, he would have slapped me. He's a nasty drunk, and I hope never to set eyes on him again."

Brett sat for a few moments, considering the information Jacqui had shared.

"That's not how he says the night ended. He told everyone in the pub that you're a real raver. They've been dining on it for days."

Jacqui gaped. "You believed him? Didn't you defend me? I've lived here for months, and you took the word of this bloke talking himself up in the pub! You don't know me if you think I would pay for a meal with a roll in his bed."

He rose from the table and paced from one end of the kitchen to the other. "He says that there is a mole on your left nipple."

Jacqui leapt to her feet. She ripped off her T-shirt, unhooked her bra, and bared her breasts.

"Look, damn you. Can you see a mole?"

An expression that she couldn't name crossed Brett's face. Her face flushed bright red; she clipped her bra and slid the T-shirt back over her head. She turned to walk away. He grabbed her by the shoulders and spun her towards him. There was no mistaking the expression now; he was livid.

"I am not your brother or your father. If that happens again, you will be flat on your back with me on top of you."

She covered her face with her hands.

"I'm sorry, sometimes I..."

"Just get carried away. Yeah, I know."

He shook his head in despair, and, sliding a hand into her hair, he tugged. She raised her face and looked into his eyes. The only thing in his eyes this time was desire. He bent his head, and she met his lips with a sigh. He held her in place with his fingers laced through her hair and deepened the kiss. He nipped at her bottom lip and slid his tongue across her lips, and she opened her mouth to allow his tongue access to explore her mouth. He pulled her against him, and his hand followed the curve of her back to delve into her shorts. Both hands cupped her bottom, and she groaned. She slid her fingers beneath the edge of his shirt, running them over the smooth muscles of his chest and shoulders. His hands snaked into her knickers, and she moaned.

Her brain was no longer functioning; she felt as though an electric jolt had zapped her. Her pulse thudded in her veins, and her heart thumped. She revelled in the feel of Brett's satiny skin and the solid muscles of his back and shoulders. She wanted to lick him; she was sure his skin would taste as good as it felt. He smelled of soap and sweat, and a morning spent working outdoors. It was a natural scent, and she curled herself against him, wanting more.

With a groan, he moved away and stepped backwards. He jammed his hands into the pockets of his jeans as he put distance between them. She swayed momentarily, refocusing her eyes, which made her sleepy with desire. His breathing was ragged, and she realised he wanted her as much as she wanted him.

"Why did you stop?" she whispered.

"Trust me; I want nothing more than to carry you to bed. The problem is I have no protection."

Jacqui groaned.

"Look, Jac, I've kept my feelings to myself, so I didn't ruin everything. Hearing about your so-called date just unhinged me; put it down to jealousy. I want you, but not if it's not for keeps. I don't want a quickie that ruins everything we already have. Tell me later about what you decide."

Jacqui's words bubbled in her throat, and she drew a large breath. It would prove nothing if she shouted at him now, but it might be a near thing.

"I went out with that jerk because you hadn't shown any interest in me. You've spent every waking moment since the attack being rude. How was I supposed to guess that you have feelings other than disgust when you glare at me? I've tried to work out what I did wrong. You've treated me like dirt, and now you tell me you're interested?"

Brett rubbed a hand across the back of his neck.

"God, I couldn't believe my luck when you entered my life. At first, I was careful; I didn't want to scare you away. If I pressured you, you might decide to tackle the road to Lonsdale daily. There must be accommodation to suit you, and I wouldn't see you anymore. Then, after the attack, I was sure you were preparing to leave, which scared me because I care about you. I decided that if you were going to leave, the sooner, the better. I was hoping you left before you broke my heart. Sid said I should apologise and tell you how I felt, but you went out with that bloke before I dared to talk to you."

"Did you think to share any of this with me? I was going crazy trying to figure out what was wrong, but I'm warning you. I'll keep my distance until after we shop in Lonsdale, but all bets are off once we return from shopping."

He gave a cheeky grin and said, "So now you've warned me, but sweetie, I'm up for the challenge."

# Chapter Eighteen

Cloistered in her study, Jacqui looked for tomorrow's tests. The paperwork that should have been in the folder wasn't. Had they fallen out of the file, or had she not included them with the rest of the paperwork? She closed her eyes, trying to visualise where they had been in the classroom. In her mind's eye, she could see the file sitting on the room's front desk. Drat! She needed the original paperwork to make copies for all the students. Should she wait until tomorrow to copy the papers? No, she needed to complete it tonight because preparing in the morning was always tricky.

As she glanced out the window, Jacqui realised it had grown dark. With a sigh, she walked along the hallway into Brett's office. He was working on the never-ending paperwork generated by the farm.

"Brett, the test papers for the kids tomorrow are still at school. I'm just going to duck into town and grab them." Distracted by the office work, he nodded and waved as she left.

New security lights, installed during the school's refit, illuminated the grounds. Jacqui was glad not to walk into the school grounds in the pitch dark. The thought of the snakes they could have disturbed during the constant mowing and gardening sessions made her skin crawl. Jacqui unlocked the main door and flicked the light switch. The file was on the front desk. She remembered putting it down to talk to a parent and then, distracted by a commotion in the playground, had not returned to pick it up. I might print these now, she thought.

While waiting for the photocopier to produce the paperwork, she scanned the classroom, satisfied. As she turned to check the copy, a noise behind made her wheel around, but nobody was there. The outside door slammed just as she had convinced herself that she had imagined the sound. The room needed blackout curtains to block out streetlight, but Jacqui could buy them later.

"Who's there?"

There was no response. Satisfied now that her imagination wasn't playing tricks, she rang Brett. When he answered the phone, she whispered, "There's somebody here, but there's no answer when..."

Her voice trailed away. The intruder staggered into the room.

He was the customer from the pub who had called her a whore. Larger than she remembered, he was unkempt and frightening. Tonight, as on the other two occasions, their paths had crossed, her abuser was intoxicated. A shiver of fear ran along her back, and butterflies crawled around her stomach. Jacqui wiped her sweating palms on the legs of her jeans. Her heart raced, and a chill swept through her body. She took a bracing breath and said,

"You are trespassing on government property. If you don't leave, I'll call the police."

Even though he laughed, the sound had no humour, and her fear escalated.

"By the time the cops arrive, I'll be gone. Since you're putting out all over town, I thought I'd try you out myself; show you what a real man is like instead of those boys you've been doing."

"I haven't been with anyone in this town. Peter is a liar who fabricated a story to cover up a night spent in the lockup, and Brett is my landlord, with no sex involved. Now get out before I scream!"

"Go ahead, girlie; no one will pay any attention." He lunged, grabbed her arm, and pulled her towards him. Jacqui twisted, trying to free her arm, but to no avail. She was too small to match his strength. This conflict would not end well. After taking a deep breath, she let out a bloodcurdling scream. With his free hand, he slapped her across the cheek, hissing,

"Shut up, bitch!"

Jacqui's face was on fire, and her head pounded with the force of the slap. He now had her pulled up against his chest. She pulled her head back and slammed it into his forehead. The headbutt was effective; he let her go and staggered backwards. Jacqui ran for the door, but he grabbed her hair just as she reached it, and excruciating pain ripped through her scalp. He pulled her further into the room and pushed her against a wall. As she collided with the wall, Jacqui let her body go limp and then flung her knee towards his groin. He caught her leg before she made contact and punched her in the face. Jacqui collapsed on the floor, and the man was on her in seconds. With a tug, he ripped her shirt down over her shoulders to pin her arms to her sides and expose her lacy bra. With a nasty laugh, he said,

"Look at those bad boys."

He destroyed her bra with a swift swipe, and she lay helplessly on the floor with her breasts exposed to him. A shudder of revulsion wracked Jacqui's body, and when he bit her, she cried out.

"Like that, do you, missy?"

"God, no! Get off me, you oaf."

"Not likely, whore. I intend to spend lots of time getting to know you."

Jacqui was hurting, unable to move and desperate for Brett to arrive. The assailant pulled Jacqui towards him and undid her jeans. She wriggled and writhed, trying to stop him from removing her clothes. He yanked her jeans and knickers off together, and Jacqui whimpered.

"Please don't do this. Please, leave me be."

"Lie still; you might even enjoy it."

Jacqui wriggled and bucked, trying to prevent him from pushing her legs apart, and he bent and bit her on the stomach. Tears welled in her eyes, and she screamed. When he straddled her legs, she was helpless.

He intended to rape her, and there was no way to prevent the attack. Fighting back had only escalated his brutality. There was no escaping this nightmare. He had immobilised her arms, and he lay jammed between her legs. With a shuddering breath, she fixated on the spot on the ceiling. Her mind drifted away, and she focused on the cracks and bumps on the roof.

Even the noises at the door didn't end her detachment.

"Police, step away from the girl. Put up your hands."

"Get off now!" shouted the police officer.

"Bugger this," said another voice.

Brett shoved past Trent and, grabbing the assailant by the collar, pulled him off Jacqui. He hauled the man to his feet and pulled his arm back to deliver a knockout punch. Trent grabbed his arm to prevent the blow from landing.

"Stop, Brett. Please don't give him anything that could be used to lessen this charge. Let me handle this; you help Jacqui."

Trent approached the assailant, who lay on the ground where Brett had dropped him. He used his foot to nudge the assailant. When the man groaned and sat up, Trent put the handcuffs on and dragged him to his feet.

Brett disappeared and returned with a sheet from the sick bay. He freed Jacqui's arms, and she lay immobile on the ground, her eyes unfocused and her face devoid of expression. He patted her on the cheeks.

"Sweetheart, it's over now. You're safe."

He wrapped the sheet around her and rocked her on his lap. She turned her face into his chest as the tears began. Tremors racked her body, and Brett felt more inadequate than ever before. What could he do to help? The best he could do for now was murmur gentle words and run reassuring hands across her back in soothing motions.

The wail of sirens and a flurry of activity outside the door preceded the two ambulance officers as they rushed into the room. Brett yelled, "Get over here and check Jacqui when they stopped beside the handcuffed man; she's the victim!"

As the ambulance pulled away from the school, a sense of déjà vu swept over Brett. He had seen more than enough ambulances for a lifetime.

# Chapter Nineteen

Brett refused to leave Jacqui's side during the ambulance ride to the hospital. The medics didn't treat her injuries but instead gave her a sedative and watched her vital signs. Their concern was that by treating her injuries, they might destroy or contaminate evidence.

At the hospital, the orderlies wheeled the stretcher away, leaving Brett alone to blame himself for an incident he could have prevented. If only he had gone with her, this wouldn't have happened. Time crawled by, and waiting was a misery. After forty minutes, he decided he needed to talk to someone about the attack. Jacqui's parents needed to know about the attack, but he couldn't tell them since he didn't have their contact details. In a moment of clarity, it occurred to him that Sid lived on the outskirts of Lonsdale, and he could talk to him. He rang, hoping that he was home and not in bed.

"Hello, this is Sid."

"Hi, it's Brett here. Have you got a minute to talk? I realise it's late, but I want to talk to you."

"Sure, go ahead."

He had barely finished telling the other man that Jacqui was in the hospital when Sid said, "Give me twenty minutes to get there. I won't be long."

It bemused Brett; one minute, he was talking to Sid, and the next, he was listening to the silence at the other end of the line. After a glance at his watch, he calculated Sid's arrival time. He looked forward to the company and someone to share his fears with.

A little over twenty minutes later, Sid bustled into the waiting room. The two men shook hands, and Sid looked at the younger man's drawn face.

"What happened?"

Sid listened as Brett relayed as much detail as he had collected, concern showing on his face when Brett began the last sentence with "If only." Sid stopped him.

"Stop, mate. Do you think Jacqui will blame you? You don't know her well if you believe she will blame you. She won't look back in a week or a month and say, "This was your fault." The blame lies with the animal that attacked her."

Another fifteen minutes passed before the doctor emerged from the room where the nurses had taken Jacqui.

"Who is the next of kin here?" he asked.

"I am. I'm Jacqui's fiancé."

The doctor walked Brett away from where Sid sat.

"Your fiancé is under mild sedation. With a broken nose, the facial bruising and swelling are extensive. The nose may require surgery later, but we can leave it as it is for now. We administered antibiotics and will test for STDs when she feels better. Are there any questions?"

"What about pregnancy?"

"We've dealt with that; I prescribed the morning-after pill, and she has already taken the medication."

Sid studied Brett when the doctor walked away.

"I thought you were a straight talker, but you lied to that doctor without a hint of guilt. Unless you are her fiancé, in which case I must offer my congratulations."

Brett looked sheepish. "I didn't know if he would tell us the extent of her injuries if I said I was her landlord and you were a friend."

Jacqui had curled up on the bed when he walked into the room. The medical staff had an IV connected to her arm, and she had her head averted from the door. He walked around the bed and looked at her face. One of her eyes had swollen shut, and he understood the doctor's comment about the bruising and swelling was an understatement. A large gash on her swollen cheek was from the ornate ring her attacker had worn. His stomach clenched, and a low moan escaped his mouth;

her lovely face looked grotesque, and she looked frail and vulnerable, lying in the fetal position.

"Oh, Jac," he groaned.

At the sound of his voice, she stirred. She tried to open her eyes, but the swelling from her broken nose was extensive, and the effort proved too much. He moved to the side of her bed and held her hand.

"It's okay, sweetheart; you're safe now."

She sighed and whispered, "Don't leave me."

"I won't leave you, but Sid is here. He's worried, too. Can he come in for a minute?"

She made a noise that he assumed was consent, so he stuck his head out of the room to invite Sid to come in. Sid's face lost all colour as he gazed at her damaged face.

"Hi, sweetie. I will find an unbruised part of your face to kiss you, okay?"

She managed a grimace that masqueraded as a smile. Sid leaned forward and kissed her near her ear.

"Few options there," he said.

When the nurse checked on Jacqui later, Brett was asleep on the bed. He'd wrapped his arms around her, and she held his hand like a lifeline. The older man had left. The nurse decided not to wake Jacqui to administer additional sedation. She clicked the light off and closed the door behind her.

Sid arrived early the following day.

"Jac, Brett has just left. He needed to go home to feed the animals and collect clothes for you to wear home this afternoon. He will search your address book to inform your parents of the attack."

Sid was an amusing visitor, and Jacqui relaxed in his presence. He spoke of inconsequential things, and she didn't need to concentrate hard on the flow of the conversation. Sid didn't expect her to make comments, so they passed the morning peacefully.

Later in the day, Brett arrived. Sid's visit had cheered Jacqui somewhat, although it would be a long time before her facial injuries healed. One eye was swollen shut, and the other was partially open, but she tried to smile when she heard his voice. He kissed her on the forehead and took hold of her hand.

"The doctor said you could go home. They will send antibiotics and painkillers; take them as directed. He suggested you rest for a few days. He's written a medical leave certificate for you for the next four weeks. I rang your parents, and they are on their way. I bought clothes for you, too."

"Can you find a nurse to help me dress?" she asked.

# Chapter Twenty

When they arrived home, Brett carried Jacqui up the veranda steps and put her in a chair in the kitchen. She had complained that she was not at death's door, but he refused to relent and carried her inside. He fussed over her, providing a cup of tea and biscuits for afternoon tea.

"What should I cook for dinner?"

She smiled and then grimaced as the bruises made their presence felt.

"Ouch, that hurts. Are you nervous? Don't worry. They will focus on my injuries; it won't matter what's for dinner."

"Jac, Sid said not to say this, but it has to be said once. When you said you were driving back into town, I heard you, but it didn't register properly. I should have paid attention instead of being caught up in my paperwork. It's hard to forgive myself when it's clear that the scumbag wouldn't have attacked you if I had been there. Jac, I'm sorry."

Jacqui stood up and walked over to where Brett sat. His head was bent, guilt and shame overwhelming him. She placed her hands on his face and tilted his head up so he could look at her. She leaned forward and kissed him. The kiss was a gentle brush of her lips against his.

"You are not to blame for what happened. The responsibility lies with the degenerate who attacked me. I couldn't have made it through last night without you. You are my anchor, and I won't let you take any blame, so let's not discuss it again."

While she relaxed in the luxury of a full bathtub — unheard of in this drought-declared area — Jacqui tried to block out the images that kept flashing through her mind. The grip of the assailant's hands and the brutal way he punched and bit her were hard to block out. The bites on her torso stung in the hot, soapy water. She lay back, her head supported by the bath's end, and tried to empty her mind. The overwhelming fear when the attacker's intent became clear had paralysed her. He might have gone easier on her if she hadn't fought, but the thought of not putting up some resistance was never a choice. She had no intention of passively lying still while he brutalised her. Could she ever return to school without remembering what happened there?

She needed to discuss this with someone, preferably an independent person. Recalling that the attack was not something she wanted Brett to experience. That he had taken the blame for the assault was not a surprise. Talking to him about the attack would cause more guilt, and she knew what had happened was not his fault.

From the solitude of the bathroom, she heard a commotion outside the back door. The dogs barked, and the sound of car doors slamming was heard. Footsteps on the veranda heralded the arrival of visitors, and she assumed her parents had arrived. She listened to the voices as her father greeted Brett and her mother's strident voice, demanding to know where she was. There was a knock on the door, and Brett said,

"Jac, your parents have arrived."

She climbed out of the bath and groaned. The bruises and cuts on her face throbbed, and her limbs felt stiff.

"I won't be long. Can you come in here for a second?"

Brett glanced in the door and, seeing she had covered herself with a large towel, slipped inside and closed the door.

"While I get dressed, can you tell my parents how messed up my face is? Hopefully, it will be less of a shock, and Mum won't freak out."

"Okay, I can do that. Try wearing something that covers up the bite marks. That should help."

Brett returned to the kitchen, determined to ease her way.

"Jacqui has just asked me to inform you of the extensive damage to her face. With her nose broken, she has two black eyes; one has closed almost completely. The bruising is extensive, and there is some swelling. She would appreciate it if you could keep your distress under control."

When Jacqui entered the kitchen, her father talked to Brett, and her mother sat in a chair facing the door.

"Oh, dear Lord," she shrieked.

Jacqui's father had spun around at the sound of Margaret's cry and scrutinised his daughter's face. He walked over and tilted her chin up, examining her damaged face.

"He certainly did a number on your darl. If that's what we can see, what else is there that we can't see?"

Jacqui blushed and said, "There's some other stuff, but I won't bore you."

Colin wrapped his arms around his daughter, and she melted into his embrace. The close contact and sympathy undid her, and she wept. He held her with soothing words and loving strokes until the worst of the sobbing stopped.

Brett watched the interaction between Jacqui and her father. He would have thought her mother would comfort her, but the woman remained firmly attached to the chair. What kind of mother ignores the distress of her daughter? Had she no compassion? As she spoke, it confirmed his assessment.

"I said coming to the country was a bad idea. If men in the country treat women this way, this is no place for you, Jacqui. That's it; we leave in half an hour. A specialist will need to examine your face, and you will need to consult with a psychologist. I know just the right person. Pack what you need and be quick. I want to be home before dark." She put her unfinished drink in the sink and then pushed the chair in.

"Where is your room? I'll help you pack."

"Stop, mum! I am not packing, and I am not leaving now. If you need to return home before bedtime, then go now. You have seen me; you know I'm alive, so there is no reason to stay. I can drive home tomorrow when I'm ready."

Jacqui's mother appealed to her father. "Colin, please talk sense into your daughter. The sooner we get home, the sooner the doctors can repair the damage."

"Margaret, we can do nothing tonight, so we may as well enjoy Brett's hospitality and leave in the morning."

Jacqui tried to smile at her father. Both women knew the argument was over when he spoke in that quiet voice. Pleased with the outcome, she moved next to Brett. She reached out and touched his arm. He turned and winked, and, taking her hand in his, he threaded his fingers through hers. They stood shoulder to shoulder, hip to hip. She needed Brett's support if her mother didn't heed her father's mandate. Her mother glared at them, and Jacqui waited for the confrontation that didn't occur.

A knock on the door startled everyone in the kitchen. The dogs had not barked to warn of a visitor, and Jacqui knew only one person could arrive at the door without them barking. She sent a querying glance to Brett, and he shrugged and smiled. When the door opened, Sid walked in, apparently sent for by Brett as a reinforcement. He moved into the kitchen and walked around the table. He hugged her.

"Not much more space for a kiss than yesterday," Sid said. He kissed her ear and turned to speak to the others in the kitchen.

"Hi Colin, I assume this lovely lady is your wife?"

Jacqui's father introduced the two, and they shook hands. Margaret looked as though she wanted to wipe her hands after the handshake. Sid clapped Brett on the shoulder. "How are you holding up, son?"

While the two new men in her life held a quiet conversation, Jacqui watched them together. Brett couldn't find a better surrogate father than Sid. She experienced a slight glow of happiness at the substitute family the three had developed. They had grown from strangers into a supportive unit, and Jacqui would miss them both when she left the next day. Turning back to her parents, she saw the warning glance her father had given her mother, but had missed its context.

Dinner was a pleasant meal, with the earlier tension having disappeared. Brett and Sid were delightful companions, telling stories that made everyone laugh. Her father had many things in common with Sid, and the conversation was lively. At the mention of beds, they argued about who would sleep on the fold-out couch in the lounge room. Jacqui said she was small enough for the temporary bed, but Sid was having none of it. He insisted that if she didn't sleep in the spare room, leaving the double bed for her parents, he would put his swag outside with the dogs. Jacqui surrendered her hands, and Sid smiled at her reaction.

"She never can give in gracefully," said Colin.

"Amen to that!" laughed Brett.

Jacqui pleaded tiredness and retired to bed. She caught Brett's eye and sent a silent message. After excusing himself from the others, he followed Jacqui to the spare bedroom.

"I need a hug," she said. Brett moved towards her and placed his hands on her shoulders. She walked forward and buried her face in his chest. The sob he heard broke his heart. He stroked her back and made comforting noises. The words he whispered were meaningless, meant only to reassure. When the crying jag finished, she looked at him and said, "I don't want to go home. I want to stay here."

He groaned, "I don't think your mother will be okay with that. I don't want you to go either, but you need the specialists that the city can offer."

Tears welled in Jacqui's eyes.

"Hug me some more. This hug has to last for the next four weeks."

Brett tightened his grip and kissed her forehead. Panic crept through as he rested his chin on the top of her head. What if Jacqui's parents' contacts secured a transfer to a school closer to home? How would he manage without her positive attitude and enthusiasm for life? He was bereft, and she hadn't even left. While he desperately wanted to tell her to stay, that would be selfish. Tomorrow, he would have to grit his teeth and appear unconcerned as she drove away.

# Chapter Twenty-One

While Jacqui loved her parents, her mother had an inflated opinion of her worth, and her father went along to keep the peace. The thought of her daughter associating with people of the calibre of Brett and Sid didn't sit well with Margaret, and she would try to separate Jacqui from the undesirable men as soon as they returned home. Jacqui expected an argument with her mother when the time came to go back to Manwarring. The doctor had given her four weeks off, after which the bruises and bites were expected to have healed. There was ample time during those four weeks to consult a psychologist and discuss her concerns. She rolled over, pulled the blankets up, and decided to meet the challenges as they presented themselves.

The feel of a body pressing her down caused Jacqui to gasp for breath. Her lips trembled, and her body shook. A whimpering cry of distress escaped her lips, and she thrashed around on the bed, trying to dislodge her attacker. Sobs ripped through her, and her head spun. Sturdy arms grabbed her, and she struggled harder.

"Jac, wake up. You're safe now. Come on, sweetie, open your eyes."

As the voice registered, Jacqui opened her eyes. Strong arms surrounded her, and the hard, lean chest of this man she knew so well cradled her. Her breath came in shuddering gasps, and her body trembled. The noises outside the bedroom told Jacqui that she had woken the household.

"What's happening? Why is that man in your bedroom, Jacqui?"

"Please, mum, go away. I can't do this now."

Colin entered the room. "Are you okay with this, son?"

Brett nodded. "Yeah, I've got it under control. I'll stay tonight."

"That doesn't sound at all proper. I can do that if Jacqui needs someone to sleep with her."

Jacqui clung to Brett. "Please make her go away."

Brett glanced at Colin, who nodded slightly and steered the arguing woman away from the door. Brett tucked himself around her and ran his hands over her back until her breathing evened out and she dozed off.

When she opened her eyes the following day, Brett had left. Jacqui propped herself up to look at the clock on the table next to her. She groaned as the many bruises protested at her new position in the bed. Jacqui could roll over and wake when her parents woke, but Brett and Sid would be up already. She wanted to help with the feeding; it would be a long time until she could assist, and she knew her absence would make Brett's life harder. The sound of chairs scraping on the floor as the two men sat to have their early morning cuppa made her smile. She knew she needed to return to Kyogle with her parents, but would rather stay with these two men who had captured her heart. As she entered the kitchen, she attempted to smile at them both and made herself a drink.

"What are you doing, Jac?" Brett asked.

"I want to help with the cattle this morning. Don't tell me you and Sid can do it without me; I know that. It will be ages until I can help again. I'll leave a note for Mum and Dad in case they wake up and wonder where we are."

The morning hours flew. After feeding the cattle, Jacqui let the dogs off for a run, and Brett went inside to make breakfast. Everything felt ordinary; it was surreal. She would be on her way toward Kyogle in a few hours, but she had long since forgotten it was home. The farm was her home, and the other house was her parents' residence. Jacqui walked towards the house with a resigned sigh, the tantalising smell of bacon and eggs filling the air.

It was almost time to go, with most of her possessions packed into the car. Jacqui dived back into the house, hoping Brett understood the look she had given him. He followed her into the house, and so did her mother.

"What have you lost, Jacqui?" her mother asked impatiently.

"Some privacy, that's what I've lost. If you go back outside, I'm sure I'll be able to find it," Jacqui replied tartly.

"God, how will I live with her for the next few weeks?" she said.

Jacqui stepped close to Brett and said, "Do you remember you said we ought to think about where we wanted to go after you kissed me last week?"

"Yes. Have you decided?"

She wrapped her arms around his neck and said, "Yes. While I'm gone, I'll buy you a present, and I expect to use it when I get back."

Brett grinned and then pulled her close, placing a light kiss on her lips. He was gentle, aware of her bruising, and didn't want to cause her any more discomfort.

"God, I'll miss you, Jac. I can't imagine being here without you. Please come back to me."

As Colin pulled away from the farmhouse, Jacqui looked back. She waved to Brett and Sid and then turned to face the front. She wiped the tears from her eyes and blew her nose. The two men watched Colin's car drive away. Sid understood how Brett must feel; he placed his hand on Brett's shoulder.

"She'll be back, mate."

Brett gazed at the empty driveway; the memory of Jacqui's tears was a physical pain in his chest.

"That woman is a real piece of work. How can a nice bloke like Colin be married to a snob? Thank God Jacqui is nothing like her mother, or I'd have thrown her out months ago. She'll only return if her mother doesn't secure a posting elsewhere. The woman could use this attack to blackmail the Education Department into sending Jacqui to a school closer to home."

"Didn't Jacqui say she was coming back? Don't worry about something that may never happen. You've seen her stand up to her mother here, and Colin is a decent bloke who will not let her mother bully Jacqui. She's made of sterner stuff. Have faith, man!" Sid said.

Brett shook his head. Despite what Syd said, Brett worried about Jacqui's return to Kyogle. Would she come back, or would her Mother convince her to stay?

Jacqui sat in the back seat of the car. Despite the Mercedes' superior suspension, the bumpy road jolted her, and soon she ached everywhere. Jacqui's mind kept straying to the time ahead; living with her mother had always been her struggle. She and her mother were on different planets; their differences were legion.

As they travelled further south, she recognised landmarks that seemed far apart on her first trip here. They whizzed past frequently, and Jacqui feared she had relinquished control of her life. Caught up in her thoughts, she didn't realise that her father was slowing the car until her mother said,

"Colin, why are we stopping here?" "Jacqui needs a rest from all the bumping. Am I right, Jac?"

"Thanks, Dad. I need a break. Maybe we can get coffee or tea."

"It doesn't look sanitary," Margaret said, eying the older-style petrol station with a frown.

"Please yourself. Dad, do you want a drink?"

"Yeah, but I will get it. You might shock the natives. Take a walk; it might help you relax. Margaret, we are getting a drink. Do you want something?"

"Oh, okay. Get me a soft drink."

Once they resumed their trip, her mother questioned Jacqui about her living arrangements and where Sid came into the equation. Jacqui answered the questions, aware that her mother didn't approve of her living arrangement or the new men in her life.

By her mother's standards, Brett had nothing to recommend him. He owned a struggling farm and had no other source of income. Brett's means of transport was an old ute and a four-wheeler. Margaret let Jacqui know her opinion that he was not a suitable partner.

"Goodness knows why you are mixing with no-hopers. I introduced you to many young, professional men, but you didn't get to know them. From your familiarity with that farmer, he is more than a friend. Why on earth did you start a relationship with him? Everyone in the town must talk about you. I'm appalled at your brazen behaviour."

Colin opened his mouth to speak when Jacqui intervened.

"Can I answer that question, please, Dad?" He looked at her in the rear-view mirror and nodded.

"When I first got to Manwarring, the shops had all closed. The only place open was the pub. I presumed I might need to stay there until I found something better, but the publican refused to rent me a room because he said sheilas cause trouble. The only other accommodation offers came from drunken customers who all offered me room and board for favours. Must I spell out the favours they offered, Mum? I was hungry, tired and facing the torture of driving on that poor excuse for a road to find somewhere to stay in Lonsdale. Brett came out just as I prepared to leave. He looked decent; his offer was without strings, and I was desperate. After staying with him for months, I have come to know that he is honest, and the living arrangement suits me. The older man, as you call him, is a friend we made through the farm. After his wife died, he dedicated his time to rescuing and rehoming working dogs. He is a lovely man who cares for both Brett and me. As for my relationship with Brett, he has a sense of humour; he is kind and decent. The blokes you thought worthy of my affections were so self-centred that they left no room for humour or integrity."

Colin laughed. "That sums up that. Margaret, if you look beyond the clothes and possessions, you will see that the two men who befriended our daughter are genuinely good blokes. I approve of them."

Margaret made a sound of disbelief, but Jacqui said,

"Thanks, Dad."

Jacqui's spirits plummeted as they drove into Kyogle late in the afternoon. She had forgotten the estate's pretentious nature and wondered how her father had managed to live here. Her mother wanted to call in favours from medical friends as soon as they arrived.

"Please, leave it until tomorrow. A day won't make any difference to the bruises." Her mother tutted in disapproval but, on this point, conceded to Jacqui's wishes. As she lay in bed that night, memories of the attack again plagued Jacqui. If only she hadn't stayed and photocopied the work, she would have left before her drunken attacker made it as far as the school.

The memory of his rough hands and body odour had her reaching for the lamp beside the bed. She couldn't lie on her bed without imagining him on top of her. Whenever she moved, pain from the bites and bruises caused her to wince. While her mother was concerned that her facial bruising might damage her aesthetic appeal, the doctors worried about bites or penetration problems. She needed to undergo more tests for hepatitis and sexually transmitted diseases, and later, there would be a trial. Recounting her assault to perfect strangers in a courtroom made her feel ill.

Unsettled by her fantasies and unable to sleep, Jacqui climbed out of bed. She slipped on a robe and made her way down the stairs. When she reached the kitchen, the light was on. Her Dad sat at the table with his head in his hands. His shoulders slumped, and he looked a picture of despair. As she walked in, he looked up at her.

"Can't you sleep, sweetie?"

"No, you too?" Jacquie said.

"Come and sit with me. Do you want a drink?" Colin said, waving a bottle of beer.

Jacqui smiled. "I didn't know you drank beer."

"Sometimes a bloke has to drink a beer or two to make everything make sense. The trouble is that I don't have enough beer to make sense of what happened to my little girl."

She held out her hand to her dad. He clasped her hand and said, "Can you get past this?"

Jacqui choked back a sob. "I'm afraid. It's not just the doctors; there's also the possibility that they will need to break my nose again. I will have to meet that animal and tell the whole sordid story to a roomful of strangers."

"God, I wish I could take your place."

She leaned forward and kissed him on the cheek.

"Where did you say the beer is?"

# Chapter Twenty- Two

Margaret spent the next week hassling acquaintances and calling in favours, wanting the best plastic surgeons in the country to examine Jacqui. After the third appointment, Jacqui refused to go to any more.

"There is no need for a fourth or fifth opinion on the bruising or my broken nose. The bruising will subside; we need to be patient. The plastic surgeons say the same thing as the Lonsdale ER doctors. It is a waste of time to visit more doctors. I'm sick of being paraded around and will not visit another doctor!"

Jacqui stormed from the room and slammed her bedroom door closed. It was a mistake to let her parents whisk her away from the farm and all it held. Resolving to stay no longer than her sick leave, Jacqui would return to Manwarring, her job, her home on the farm, and a new relationship.

With her point made clear to her mother, Jacqui knew she should investigate counselling sessions with a psychologist. Jacqui broached that subject after dinner. Margaret said she knew the best person to see. She felt uneasy about using her parents' contacts, but since sessions were supposed to be confidential, she gave in and let her mother book the appointment.

After speaking with the psychologist, Jacqui felt relieved and booked an appointment for later in the week. Sue, the doctor, walked through to reception to greet her mother, who insisted on driving her and waiting.

"Hello, Sue. How did it go today?" asked Margaret.

"We did well, didn't we, Jacqui? We discussed the attack and the impact and..."

"Stop! My information is confidential. There will be no more appointments if you discuss this with my parents."

After glancing at Margaret, Sue looked abashed and said, "I'm sorry. We achieved a great deal in our session; I lost myself in the moment. It won't happen again."

"Don't be foolish, darling. I'm your mother, and I worry about you. Sue didn't break confidentiality. It's only natural to ask Sue."

"Then it's only natural for me to find another psychologist who can respect my privacy," said Jacqui.

Reassured that the psychologist would respect her privacy, Jacqui confirmed the next appointment.

The highlight of Jacqui's day was her phone call after dinner each night. Brett used the speakerphone, allowing him and Sid to talk simultaneously.

One evening, Brett said, "The department is appointing a temporary teacher to cover your absence. I remember how difficult it was for you to find somewhere to stay, so I've offered her the spare room. Is that okay?"

"Do you want to pack my stuff and let her use my room?"

Brett said, "Are you coming back?"

"Yes, of course I am!"

"Good, then she can stay in the spare bedroom."

A great sadness overcame her each evening when the call ended, and Jacqui felt a deep sense of longing for home. She missed life on the farm and the two men who had recently become part of her life. Homesickness had not been a problem when she moved to Manwarring, but now the flutters and pains in her stomach tormented her.

While in the city, she intended to go shopping. She needed working clothes —jeans, shirts, boots, and an Akubra-style hat. It took her longer than she expected to find the right clothes. The shops displayed acres of jeans and casual shirts, but Jacqui needed essential gear. Designer jeans and flashy shirts weren't suitable, so she abandoned the boutiques and searched for a large chain store. People who had passed gawked at her, while others tried to be more discreet. She realised that her facial bruising still drew people's attention. Her face was a kaleidoscope of colour since the attack. At first, the bruises were a purplish-black, and as time passed, they changed to a greenish hue; now, they were a light brown.

This week marked the third week of her sick leave; she wanted to go home, but she knew she couldn't teach again if her face still showed extensive bruising. On impulse, Jacqui walked to the makeup counter and spoke to the consultant about cover-up makeup. After discussing Jacqui's requirements, a sales consultant took pity on her and offered to apply the makeup, so she knew how much to use as a concealer. The results were astounding, achieved through trial and error, and Jacqui was ecstatic. The vast smile she gave the sales assistant lit up her face.

That night, she phoned Brett, only to hear the phone ring out. Her eyebrows drew together. Where was he? Her mouth went dry, and her pulse picked up as her mind raced to the worst-case scenario. Had there been an accident? Please don't panic, she counselled herself. There could be a simple excuse for his absence. Did he drive home with Sid? After three weeks of helping, Sid wanted to return home. Comforted by this thought, she dialled Sid's number. After waiting for a few seconds, he picked up the phone. They chatted for a few minutes, exchanging news and discussing the weather, and then she asked if Brett was there; he wasn't.

When Sid left, Brett intended to finish his job and settle in for the night. After completing her call, she redialed Brett's number. There was still no response. Mystified, Jacqui turned in for the night.

# Chapter Twenty-Three

After Sid left, Brett caught up on the office work. He liked this part of the job least, but knew he couldn't get out of it with his mum gone. Sid left sooner than he intended, and Brett suspected his friend didn't care for Chloe any more than he did.

Reflecting on the visit, Brett realised he had lucked out. Not only were Jacqui and Sid honest and truthful, but Sid also demonstrated integrity in his dealings with both of them. To trust two people with his affection was a novel experience for him.

Deciding to tackle his emails first, he set aside the less enjoyable accounts and stock forecasts for later. An email from Jacqui appeared, and his heart soared with joy, as she had sent him a message today, even though they had spoken the night before. When he opened the e-mail, the smile froze on his face. According to Jacqui, she had found Mr Right. While attending a fundraiser that day, she met the man her mother said was out there. Brett looked at the letter in disbelief. She appeared happy when they talked last night and looked forward to returning to the farm. How could this be possible? He grabbed the phone to ring and sort this out. One sentence said, 'This decision was hard for me to make, and if you care for me, you will respect my choice. Please don't call me; we will gain nothing by discussing my choice, which prevented him from making the call.

Pain sliced through his body, almost bringing him to his knees. He felt shattered, crushed by Jacqui's desertion. With their relationship ended, his stomach felt hollow. How could she do this to him? He remembered her promise to buy him a present to use when she returned. The unexpected breakup gave him both physical and mental pain. Despite the plea not to contact her, Brett picked up the phone. Why would she question if he cared for her? Bowing his head, he replaced the receiver. Jacqui didn't want to talk to him, so he should respect her request. A powerful urge to ring and beg her to reconsider surged through him, but he needed to survive this breakup with his pride intact.

Mindful that he needed to get up, he drank a few beers and returned home. Even though he rarely drank, he headed for the pub that night to consume enough alcohol to blunt the edges of his despair. He heard the phone ring as he walked from the shed to the house. Brett jogged from the shed in case Jacqui changed her mind and called him. When he entered the kitchen, it was in time to see Chloe hang up the phone.

"Who was that?" Chloe started at the sound of his voice.

"Ah, just a wrong number," she said, shrugging.

With Chloe living in the house, Brett had company. The problem was that she wasn't Jacqui. It wasn't fair to compare the two girls, and he knew it, but he couldn't stop himself. Chloe had designs on him and fluttered around, touching him and flirting. Brett had become caught in a trap of his own making. Never again would he offer to help someone out; it backfired on him twice. When Jacqui returned, he expected the department to transfer Chloe. Now, without her return, the annoying woman wasn't going anywhere.

Chloe wasn't a restful companion. She grumbled about the dogs and their daily habit of lying on the veranda. Complaints about the heat, the dust, and the kids at school became repetitive. Brett knew she had been harassing the dogs when he was not there, and he took them with him whenever possible.

When she bought the answering machine, he expressed surprise. Her explanation that they missed calls while at work sounded logical enough. The number of messages they received disproved her need for an answering machine. Brett checked the device each evening, but neither Jacqui nor Sid left a message. Sid, taking sides and supporting Jacqui's decision, caused Brett more heartache. With no contact from either of them, his mood spiralled downward. While he should have been buoyant, he felt dispirited. After the recent rain, he had grass growing in the paddocks, and he only fed the cattle supplements weekly instead of daily, but even that didn't make him smile. To add to his misery, Brett discovered Chloe considered she had no obligation to do any housework. Brett went back to eating sandwiches and tins of food. It didn't appear to bother Chloe what she ate, but then he discovered that a catering mob from Lonsdale delivered food to the school. Brett was livid.

Since Jacqui left, the joy leeched out of his life. Brett dragged himself out of bed in the morning and plodded through his tasks, which, until recently, he had worked with enthusiasm and optimism. Jacqui's presence was too good to be true, but as time passed, Brett believed in his good fortune and thought his life would pan out. His judgment was flawed; how did he not see this coming? Would Brett be alone for the rest of his life? He decided it was better to be alone than risk this pain again.

# Chapter Twenty-Four

Jacqui rose early and used the makeup concealer she had brought the previous day. Today was her last appointment with the psychologist, and she had packed and was ready to leave. The thing that worried her most was her inability to contact Brett. An answering machine replaced the never-ending ring of his phone. Further concerning her was the message on the answering service. The recorded voice said,

"Hi, this is Chloe speaking. Brett and I can't come to the phone. Leave a message, and we'll ring you back." Slightly angry that the supply teacher had made herself right at home, Jacqui left a message. Brett did not ring back. Jacqui pushed the worry aside. She collected her bag and said goodbye to her mother as she walked out to her mother's new Audi. It was a flashy car for the suburbs, but Jacqui liked its quick pickup and easy handling.

She remained upbeat and happy as the receptionist escorted her into the doctor's office.

"Jacqui, you look well today," said Sue.

"An excellent makeup artist helped me cover the bruises. I wish I'd thought of it sooner. Instead of having people stare, I could have used makeup weeks ago."

"What are your plans now that we have nearly finished our sessions?"

"Nearly finished? As far as I knew, this was our last appointment, and then I intend to go home to the farm."

"At the moment, you need clearance to resume work. I don't think your emotional recovery is conducive to returning so soon. I need to see you again once a week for the next few weeks. After that, we can reassess, and if I believe you will be all right, I'll give you the clearance you need to return to work."

"You have to be kidding me! I'm okay now, and I want to go home." Jacqui's temper was rising, and she flushed with the effort of not shouting at the woman.

"That's interesting. You have twice called a place you have lived in for a few months 'home.' Perhaps you must decide if you must return or need a space here where your parents can support you."

"I don't want to stay in this town, and I don't need my parents to care for me. My job is in a remote town. I harassed every politician I knew to get repairs made, and I want to go back and enjoy the results of my efforts."

"I'm sorry, but I can't give you a clearance yet."

Jacqui stormed from the room. Her eyes welled with tears, and she wanted to stamp her feet and throw a tantrum for the first time since her arrival. What more was she supposed to do? She had attended all the sessions and discussed her issues with Sue, so the woman's refusal to grant medical clearance was unjustified. She was sure she was all right to go; staying in Kyogle with no job and her friends at work made no sense.

Her mother's demeanour sent off warning signals when she arrived home. She feared that her mother and Sue were manipulating her, but was unsure what to do. She rang Brett, needing to hear his voice, but she reached the answering machine again. "Damn you, Brett! Turn off this stinking answering machine. Pick up, please. I need to speak with you," she said. The lack of response made the problem seem worse.

Although not one to sulk, Jacqui spent the next two days in her bedroom. At first, she spent her time catching up on reading the newest novels she had purchased and that she still hadn't opened. Tired of reading, she logged onto the education website and downloaded programs and resources for the national curriculum, the government's newest tool.

There wasn't any point in using makeup to conceal the bruises. Who would see her in the house? Her skin had a yellowish tinge that she would cover with makeup when she returned to school. Walking back into the room where the attack happened would be difficult, but she needed to overcome her nerves to keep her teaching position. If she enlisted Brett's help, he might walk around the school with her. She wanted to leave and go back to the farm.

Jacqui resolved to fix the uncertainty that dogged her. After ringing around, she found a psychologist available. Jacqui made an appointment with a woman who had recently moved into the area and had not yet established a client list. The meeting was only two days away, and she used those two days to get her life back in order. Jacqui rang the department to provide an update and suggest a possible start date. After organising a medium-sized SUV rental, she packed the things she had left behind from her first move to Manwarring.

Jacqui's mother noticed a change in her daughter's temperament and observed her packing with apprehension. Jacqui was getting ready to leave, but Margaret hoped they might postpone or prevent her return, having put the two blockers in her way.

Margaret was sure she knew what was best for Jacqui, and this infatuation with a poor farmer was not part of her plans for her daughter. She was confident Jacqui would settle if she found the right doctor or lawyer, someone of substantial means and high standing in the community. Margaret wanted grandchildren and the bragging rights that Jacqui's prestigious marriage would allow her. She wished to tell her compatriots, "My son-in-law, the doctor (slash lawyer)." Even though Margaret married a banker, she wanted better for her daughter, and a hick farmer wasn't it. The two roadblocks she had put in place were for Jacqui's benefit.

Jacqui was ready to leave to visit the new psychologist when Margaret called out to her.

"Where are you going, Jacqui?"

"Just in town."

"Why don't you wait for me, and I'll come too?"

"Sorry, mum, I have to run. See you later."

Margaret stood at the window watching her daughter drive away in the rented SUV. Were her plans unravelling? She decided she needed to shore up her position and rang Sue.

"Are you sure Jacqui can't start without a release from you?" she asked with no preamble.

"Hello, Margaret. I'm sure she can't start without a release. The education department won't risk taking on a teacher suffering post-traumatic stress, which I diagnosed her with having."

Although reassured, Margaret paced as she waited for her daughter to return; she needed to know what she was doing.

Jacqui weaved the SUV through the local traffic of Kyogle and out onto the freeway. The appointment at the psychologist's new room was only a short drive away. The suburb had undergone a renewal and had grown since she was last here. Jacqui's surroundings made her feel comfortable when she entered the doctor's office. Unlike Sue's practice, this one displayed no valuable art on the walls, no glass coffee tables with large glossy magazines, and no snooty receptionist. The friendly receptionist looked up as Jacqui surveyed the room.

"Can I help you?"

"Hi, I'm Jacqui, and I booked an appointment at two o'clock."

"Doctor won't be long if you'd like to take a seat."

A few minutes later, a trim lady appeared at the door. She smiled and ushered Jacqui into her room.

"Hello, I'm Toni. What can I do to help you?"

Jacqui's composure shattered. Tears rolled down her face as she told of the attack. When her tirade finished, the doctor looked at her with pursed lips. She explained that it seemed the other doctor was acting on her mother's instructions rather than caring for her.

"What you're suggesting is malpractice. The accusation is a severe matter."

"I don't want to get anyone into trouble; I want my life back. If I become your patient, could you please request the notes from the other doctor? You could tell if she was deliberately trying to delay me. If you're happy with my notes and progress, could you release me to go back to work?"

Toni took the details of the other practitioner and asked if Jacqui remembered any of the dates. She pulled out her mobile phone and went to the organiser. Toni jotted down notes of the dates and times of the appointments.

"If you wait a minute, I will get my receptionist to contact the other doctor and ask if I can talk to her."

The receptionist knocked on the door a few moments later to say that Sue Wright was on the phone. Jacqui listened to the conversation; this was her life they were discussing. Much to her surprise, Toni's voice rose, and a look of anger crossed her face.

"The patient can change practitioners, and as her new doctor, I am free to ask for her files. It will only take a few minutes to contact the AMA's hotline, and they will order you to hand over the data."

Toni listened for a moment and then replied,

"Those files need to be in my office early tomorrow morning, or I will take this further. Send them by courier." Toni hung up and looked at Jacqui.

"I hate to say this, but I suspect your misgivings from that conversation are correct. Can you come in tomorrow at eleven? The files should have arrived by then. It will give me enough time to review them. We can go from there."

Jacqui beamed at her, happy for the first time since Sue pronounced her unfit to return to work.

# Chapter Twenty-Five

When Jacqui returned home, she discovered that her mother was furious with her. Sue had rung to say that Jacqui had consulted another doctor, and there was no alternative but to hand over the files. She confided to her friend that the other doctor might immediately release Jacqui to work based on the notes in her records. Jacqui watched, amazed, as Margaret ranted about her selfish behaviour and lack of respect.

That night, dinner was quiet. Colin was not astute in judging the level of malice in a disagreement between his wife and daughter, but eventually, the hostile atmosphere caught his attention.

"What in the devil is eating you two?

Jacqui looked at her mother. "Will you tell him of your underhandedness, or will I?"

For the first time, Colin looked concerned. Margaret hadn't intended to tell him what she had done, but she decided it was best to get in first.

"Jacqui is so ungrateful that it boils my blood." When Jacqui did not comment, Margaret became encouraged and continued.

"When she came home, I approached all of my connections. She had the chance to have the best treatment that money could buy. What does she do? She refuses to go to another doctor who could help with the bruising on her face."

"The bruising looks okay, Margaret. The first doctor told us it would take time for the bruising to disappear. I don't see why you insisted on dragging her to others only to hear the same thing."

"Just because you don't understand doesn't make it wrong. I get a top psychologist to treat her, and today I discovered she has gone to another doctor and insisted that Sue surrender her notes."

Her father looked at Jacqui and said,

"Was there a reason you went somewhere else, Jac?"

"Dad, Sue Wright revealed to Mum how the seasons were going. When we started, I asked her to respect my privacy. Even though I'm ready to return to work, she won't release me for at least two more weeks. I wanted a second opinion because I'm sure she is holding me here, so mum is happy."

"Margaret, have you been interfering with Jacqui's treatment?"

"Colin, you don't understand. I never wanted Jacqui to be a teacher, and now we are picking up the pieces after she has experienced an assault. She needs to be at home where we can look after her. She should be married by now, with a lovely home and babies. Is that too much to ask?"

Colin's eyes widened, and he gave a slow, disbelieving shake of the head.

"I always knew you were a snob, dear wife, but I never thought you were selfish. Jacqui should make her own decisions. This choice is hers; if she wants a second opinion, that's her prerogative. I trust her to make the right decisions, and you should trust her too."

"Thanks, Dad," Jacqui said.

The atmosphere between Jacqui and her mother remained frosty, so Jacqui returned to her bedroom after the drink. She tried Brett's phone again, but the machine answered. Admitting defeat for the moment, Jacqui rang Sid; he was always happy to talk. She told him about the problem with the doctor and her hopes for the next day. As the conversation ended, Sid said, "I guess you want to find out if I've spoken to Brett?"

"Yes, have you seen or talked to him?"

"I keep getting that dratted answering machine. What, Brett's become the president, and he must screen calls? Suddenly, he's not contactable. I don't understand why he won't talk to us. When are you coming back? If you stop here on your way through, I could go to the farm with you," Sid said.

"Okay, that's a good idea. If you drive to the farm, you'll find my car there. I can drive the rental back to Lonsdale, as they have an agency there. I'll tell you what happens tomorrow with the new psychologist. I'm optimistic that she will release me."

Jacqui arrived at the consulting rooms, eager to hear the news of her medical release. She checked the reading material and chose a magazine just as Toni left her office.

"Hi Jacqui, come on in."

Toni pulled out the file from Sue Wright when Jacqui sat in the visitor's chair.

"So, Sue complied with the request and sent the file. She told Mum that I had changed psychologists and wanted a second opinion. Mum was furious; she ranted about me being ungrateful for her help."

"Well, the file is troubling. The notes in the margin show that Sue kept your mother informed regarding your progress. Not privy to what you were saying, but aware of your emotional state."

"Well, isn't that just great? I told the woman to respect my privacy, but clearly, she doesn't understand the notion."

"From the notes, Ms Wright was comfortable to release you last week, but as a favour to your mother, agreed to hold up the release for another two weeks. From this report, I can give you the medical clearance to enable you to return to work."

Jacqui let out a whoop of joy. "Thank you, God."

Toni chuckled. "Nobody has ever called me that before. There is just one thing. You may have nerves associated with entering the building where the attack occurred. I will show you relaxation techniques to use. If you feel overwhelmed, we can talk on the phone, or you can come for an appointment."

Jacqui left the consulting rooms, a huge smile wreathing her face. Her eyes danced, and there was a bounce in her step. There were phone calls to make, one to the Education Department and one to Sid. There was no point in trying Brett. If he wanted to talk, he could have picked up the phone or replied to one of the many messages she had left. When Sid heard her voice, he knew the news was good, and it delighted him that Jacqui could return to her job and the farm.

A little unsettling was the news that, in her absence, the Education Department had placed the relief teacher on contract as the school's second teacher. With Jacqui's years of experience and senior teacher status, she would be an ideal candidate for the principal position. The paperwork and decisions were her duties. She asked for written confirmation of this decision. The public servant handling the case agreed to send an email and a formal letter.

Jacqui's departure was a cool one. The previous night, her mother tried cajoling, bribing, and bullying her to change her mind about returning. She refused each inducement until her mother finally gave up. Her father avoided her mother's intense efforts and farewelled her when he left for work.

With bags packed into the hire car, Jacqui decided an early start was better than hours of stony silence.

"Don't let it surprise you if your farmer has moved on to a newer conquest," her mother said.

Her mother's last comment unnerved Jacqui. Could Brett have formed a relationship with the new border? It appeared unlikely, but stranger things had happened. What would she do if she returned to the farm to find another woman had taken her position? Was this relief teacher the offspring of a farmer, someone able to help Brett with the farm in ways she couldn't? Did the other woman understand the stress he suffered trying to run the farm?

Brett made his intentions clear twice before the attack and before she left. Had he changed his mind? Jacqui pushed the worry aside and focused her attention on the road.

As Jacqui retraced the steps she had taken four months before, she felt a frisson of excitement. Anticipation and nervousness tinged her first trip, but this time she was eager for the journey to end. Jacqui was going home, and the thought of seeing Brett and Sid brought a smile to her face. Unused to driving long distances, she stopped twice for a drink and a walk. She was going to Sid's place first, so the time of her journey was not crucial. If she arrived late in the afternoon, she could stay with Sid and drive to the farm tomorrow morning.

The long-awaited rain had arrived while she was in the city, and the landscape's transformation was amazing. The paddocks she passed were green, and in places, the grass was lush and long. She hoped that Brett, too, had pasture for his stock. Even if the rain didn't bring immediate financial benefits, he must be happier now. At the beginning of her time, his plight seemed hopeless, as day after day the sun shone brightly, and the meteorologist predicted no rain.

Jacqui arrived at Sid's place around lunchtime, so they caught up on their news. He looked well, but she worried about him here on his own. Sid rang Brett's phone before they left, but there was no reply. With Jacqui's bags loaded in the back of Sid's ute, they arrived in Lonsdale and left the hire car at the depot.

Jacqui fidgeted in the car seat, adjusting the position and moving the sun visor. The closer they got to their destination, the more nervous she became.

"Sit still, Jac. You're making me nervous, too."

"It's hard to work out what is going on with Brett. What happened to the honest and forthright man I lived with for months? He should have told us if we did something wrong, but this silence is too much."

As they drove through the gate, her stomach twisted, and a lump formed in her throat. Although anxiety regarding their reception was present, it thrilled her that, at last, she was in the one place she called home. They had left a message on the answering machine earlier, but it was unclear if Brett had received it. The farm looked prosperous; the paddocks were adorned with green grass. Despite the prosperous look of the farm, there was an empty air about it.

A barking frenzy greeted their arrival, and Jacqui and Sid walked over to greet the dogs. When Jacqui let them off, Barney came to stand between the two adults, his whole body wagging with his enthusiastic welcome. Molly ran around them in circles, giving happy yips and rushing in for caresses. When the dogs calmed down, Sid and Jacqui walked towards the house, the dogs trailing behind them.

The kitchen door opened, and a young woman peered out. She was pleasant enough to look at, her blond curls swinging around her shoulders and her blue eyes wide and childlike. The shrewish voice that emerged from her mouth contradicted her innocent image.

"Ya mutts, shut up!" she shrieked. The dogs cringed and slunk away.

"The dogs have no water," said Sid.

"Brett will get around to it. They're a bloody nuisance. We will euthanise the old dog and sell the bitch to someone who wants a working dog. Why do we need them? I help Brett when he needs it. I guess you must be Jacqui. Brett said you were coming. Come in and get your stuff. I think he left a note for you."

Jacqui recoiled at the news that she was about to pick up her stuff.

"Pick up my stuff? Why? Is Brett here?"

"No, he got called away, and you need to pick up your stuff because he's throwing your arse out."

Jacqui chewed her bottom lip to prevent herself from crying. Why was he evicting her? Surely, he couldn't have formed a relationship with the foul-mouthed shrew? What happened to his commitment to her?

"Now you know who I am. Could I ask who you are?" Jacqui said.

"My name is Chloe Thomas, Brett's new border." She turned and walked through the door. Sid touched Jacqui's arm and gave it a squeeze of encouragement as he ushered her through the door. Although it was messier than Jacqui's kitchen, it looked the same. The room gave off a neglected air as if no one had cooked or eaten there for months. She was sad as she gazed at the house that had once been her home.

"Your belongings are in boxes in the room that was your office. I guess I don't have to show you the way."

Jacqui and Sid moved through the house and entered the office. Jacqui's heart dropped when she saw the boxes; everything she had brought to the farm was packed into cartons. On top of the closest container was an envelope with her name written in Brett's distinctive hand. With trembling fingers, she tore the envelope open and read the note. A small moan conveyed her distress; she eased herself onto the chair. When she handed the letter to Sid, he scanned it. A couple of sentences jumped out at him. 'Sorry to have it end this way' and 'No more contact between us' were two comments that struck him as unfeeling and thoughtless. He looked at Jacqui. She was trying to hold it together, but he could see the tears in her eyes.

After they loaded the boxes into the car, Jacqui returned to the house with a small wrapped present. With her hands on her hips, she glared at Chloe.

"Where is my car?"

"Brett got rid of it. Someone trashed it. When we came home, we found that someone had smashed the windscreen; it looked like someone had taken a hammer to the panels. They slashed the tyres, and Brett had to get a tow truck to remove the wreck. The money he got from the wreckers will go to your account."

"Why didn't he contact me? I had the car insured. The policy would have covered the cost of a new vehicle. Now, I have no car or money for a new one."

Chloe shrugged.

"Get mummy and daddy to buy you one. Brett says they're rich."

Chloe thrust the keys at Jacqui. "He asked me to give you these keys, but he's removed the keys to the house. What's the present?"

"It's for Brett. I'll just put it on the side table in his bedroom."

Chloe raced around the table and blocked her way as she walked towards the door.

"Leave it on the table in the kitchen. I'll make sure Brett gets it," said Chloe.

"Sorry, that will not happen. This present is personal, and I intend to leave it in his room. Get out of the way!"

She elbowed her way past Chloe and reached for the door handle. The other woman lunged at her again. As Jacqui grasped the door handle, Chloe tried to stop her from opening the door, but she underestimated Jacqui's determination. The door flung open, and Brett was sitting on the bed. He had his head in his hands, and when he raised it to gaze at Jacqui, the hurt and sadness she felt reflected in his eyes.

"Brett, please ...." Jacqui wanted to beg, but he turned his face away. She handed him the gift when she wiped the tears from her cheeks.

"I bought myself a present, but without your help, it's useless. It seems like you've struck it lucky with your new border. Maybe you'll find a use for the contents," Jacqui said as she handed him the brightly wrapped packet. With her head held high and her spine stiff, she walked out the door without looking back.

When she arrived at the ute, she realised the dogs were in the cage attached to the back of the vehicle. She spotted the dogs at the same time as Chloe.

"What are you doing with the dogs?" she shouted.

"I will save you the cost of euthanising Barney, and when Brett returns Jacqui's money for her car, I will pay him the same price he paid me for Molly," Sid replied.

Sid pulled in at a service station cum fast-food outlet on the approach to Lonsdale. He had watched Jacqui throughout the journey, and her demeanour showed that the afternoon's events had shattered her. She had travelled with her eyes closed for most of the trip; it was an avoidance tactic that prevented her from socialising with Sid.

"Come on, let's get a cuppa and stretch," said Sid.

"If it's all the same to you, I might stay in the car, thanks," Jacqui replied.

"Sorry, sweetie, that's not a choice. Let's go!"

Grumbling at what a bully Sid was, Jacqui complied with his wishes. She felt better after drinking the tea and eating hot, greasy chips smothered with gravy.

"What do I do now?" she asked as they returned to the car.

"Seems I've got a border," said Sid. Her face crumpled, and he moved over to hug her. "It will be okay, Jac; we'll manage."

# Chapter Twenty-Seven

Brett dropped his head and cradled it in his arms when the door closed behind Jacqui. Grief roared through him and would have felled him if he were standing. It was over; there was no chance she might change her mind. While she was living with him, he tried to remember the warning that if it was too good to be true, it probably was, but her constant humour and kindness made him believe that his luck had changed. When she told him she was coming back, he believed her. She said it two or three times; the last time, he told her he rented a room to Chloe, and she insisted she was coming back.

Brett thought about what had happened. Jacqui's reaction to seeing him made little sense. None of this made any sense. Chloe told him Jacqui had left a message saying she and Sid were calling in to collect her things. If that was the message she left, then why was she upset?

He heard Sid and Jacqui arrive and strained to listen to the conversation. The noise of someone moving boxes in her office filtered into his room. The raised voices suggested there was an argument, but Brett couldn't figure out the problem. There was shoving and banging outside his bedroom door, and the door burst open. His heart pounded when Jacqui walked through the door, and his pulse raced. God, he missed her.

The bruising on her face was gone, but she didn't appear well. Her face was ghostly white, and tears filled her eyes. For a breathtaking moment, Brett thought she wanted to rekindle their relationship, and his heart leapt in anticipation. The small package in her hands made his heart soar. As he watched, her face closed up. Her expression told him she was here to finish with him. He knew what it was when she thrust the little box at him. The disdain and contempt in her voice made him cringe. He was hurting, and from the tears running freely down her cheeks, it was clear she was heartbroken, too.

Brett was confused. Why was Jacqui distressed? The joke about the condoms fell flat when she ended their relationship. What did she mean when she said she hoped to use them with him? He made it plain that he didn't want a one-night stand, and by ending their relationship, that was all they could have. What happened to Mr Right? Was he not up to his responsibilities?

Brett walked out to the kitchen. Chloe was sitting at the table with a cup of tea in front of her. "Sorry, I tried to stop her, but she pushed past me. Ah, well, good riddance, I say! You don't need a snotty-nosed socialite here. I can help when you need me to," she said.

Brett moved past her without comment. He stopped when he opened the door to walk out onto the veranda.

"Where the hell are the dogs?" he growled.

Chloe fidgeted for a moment and then said, "That bloke. Sid took them both."

"Why did he do that?"

"Ah, well, I said you were considering having the old dog euthanised. That Sid fellow flipped and took both the dogs with him," Chloe said with a shrug.

"Great! You've been a big help. I have no friends, and I have to do everything on my own. Why did you tell Sid I considered having Barney euthanised when it's a lie?"

"Sorry, I was only trying to help. The old dog was useless, especially when you had to pick him up and put him in the truck. That bloke, Sid, saw you coming, and he dumped the dog on you. You should thank me instead of yelling at me," Chloe said.

With shoulders slumped, Brett walked out of the kitchen.

# Chapter Twenty-Eight

Before returning to school, Jacqui needed to replace the SUV. As she and Sid looked for a car, memories of the first time she traded her car flooded back. She convinced Sid to use another car dealership; she didn't want to buy the vehicle from the same place where she and Brett had bought her first car.

The last task she needed to complete was to visit the classroom where the attack occurred. Nausea rolled in her stomach when she thought of entering the empty school at the weekend.

Jacqui was rarely still while sitting; she bounced her foot, and Sid often caught her twisting her signet ring. She was like a wound-up clock, ready to go off. He waited for her to confide in him. When Jacqui didn't confide in him, Sid brought up the issue himself. "Jac, something is bothering you. Can you tell me what's wrong?"

"I need to return to school when the kids aren't there. The problem is that I'm scared to be in the building alone." She forced a laugh. "How foolish is that?"

"Not foolish at all. The solution is straightforward. Pick a time, and I will go with you," Sid said.

Jacqui and Sid alighted from the car. The gates to the front of the school stood wide open, and a frown crossed her face as she approached. A knot formed in her stomach as they walked towards the door of the demountable classrooms. Her pulse raced, and her hands shook. Sid reached for her hand and held it in his callused one. He squeezed her fingers, took the keys from her trembling fingers, and inserted them into the lock.

Walking into the room brought back the horror of the attack, and she took a step backward. Her stomach churned, and her voice shook. "Sid, I can't do this."

"It's okay, sweetie. We can take as much time as you need. Why not try the relaxation techniques that Toni showed you?"

With Toni's techniques, Jacqui's pulse steadied, and her hands stopped shaking. She moved around the room, stopping at the places where the assailant had attacked her. Sid studied her, ready to step in if necessary. He felt proud of her. Returning to the attack site was difficult, and she had to confront the fear and apprehension that must have been present. She turned and smiled at Sid. He breathed a sigh of relief; she would be okay.

The school term seemed unending. Jacqui found it intolerable to be working with Chloe. The woman used every excuse to discuss what she and Brett were doing. He was now a trendsetter, and he and his border dined out at least twice a week. Hearing about their social life made Jacqui angry. She feared running into Brett at the school if he drove Chloe in for any reason.

A leadership struggle ensued on her return to school. Jacqui used the department's letter to make the other woman follow directions. After evicting Chloe from her office, she rescheduled the buses that Chloe had organised to arrive at nine o'clock.

While Jacqui taught the older children, Chloe asked to work with the younger classes. Along with the ongoing fight about daily activities, Jacqui felt something was wrong with the student's reaction to Chloe. Often, she visited the junior's classroom without warning, but each time she visited, she found the other woman speaking in a sweet voice to the kids who sat in their seats like deer in the headlights. Jacqui couldn't pinpoint what was wrong, but the answer came when a mother asked for a meeting.

"Cooee, Miss Stuart, may I have a word, please?" called a petite woman. Jacqui recognised the woman as the mother of the school's only Grade 2 pupil. She walked toward the mother, smiling.

"Hello, Mrs Barnes. How can I help you?"

"If you don't mind, can we take this into your office?" Mrs Barnes said, looking over her shoulder.

Jacqui walked into the building and to her office, a bemused expression on her face. Chloe had seen the two women walk into the building and followed them.

"Do you want me to take part in this meeting? I should be here as I'm Christopher's teacher," she said.

Jacqui gritted her teeth. "I want you to oversee the bus kids. They can't be outside unsupervised while moving vehicles are near the schoolyard. I will update you later."

Mrs Barnes looked relieved when Jacqui sent the other woman away.

"This is difficult, but I can't stay quiet any longer. My Christopher cries in the morning before coming to school. I fight with him to get him onto the bus, and he has wet his bed every night for weeks. He says Miss Thomas is mean; she shouts and says mean things, frightening him. When I asked him why he didn't tell you, he said she's nice every time you come in."

Jacqui frowned. "I was sure something was off, but I couldn't catch her at it. I don't understand how she knows when I'm coming."

Mrs Barnes grimaced. "She posted a student as a lookout. The kids have to take turns."

Jacqui ran her hands through her hair as she tried to decide how to handle this issue.

"Is this fear widespread? Have you talked to other parents?"

"Yes, it's just that I was on the school run this week when I spoke to you. Next week, I'm sure someone else will tell you."

"Okay, I'd better come up with some solutions, pronto. Can you tell the other parents I'll try fixing the issue?"

When the mother left, Chloe returned to the room.

"What did she want?" she said in a rude tone.

Jacqui couldn't tell Chloe of the complaint without first investigating the grievance.

"Oh, she had questions about the curriculum and thought she should talk to the principal." Jacqui shrugged and packed up her laptop, preparing to leave.

"What? Am I not able to answer her questions? Stupid cow. She has a major crybaby as a child; he whines all the time."

As Jacqui drove up the driveway, the dogs barked a welcome. Sid walked out to greet her and watched as she unchained the dogs. He listened to her laugh, but the smile on her mouth often didn't reach her eyes. There was an inherent unhappiness that she tried hard to hide. She existed, but no longer lived with the joy she once showed. In addition, she'd experienced dramatic weight loss, and Sid worried about her. She turned to greet him and smiled at the two glasses and a bottle of wine he held in his hands. She followed him onto the veranda, the dogs on her heels, and sank into her usual chair.

"You always know what a girl wants," Jacqui said as she took the first sip.

"Nothing that a good red can't improve."

"Well, see if you can fix this. A mother came to inform me of an issue this afternoon. She told me that Chloe terrified her son. She struggles to get him on the bus in the morning, and he wets his bed at night. The child told his mother that Chloe yells at them and is mean to them. She has a guard by the door; the child's job is to tell her if anyone is coming. I suspected something was wrong, but I couldn't identify anything specific. What do I do now?"

Sid sat for a moment. "Hm, tricky. Could you tape her without her knowledge? I'm not sure what the law is."

"Even if it's unlawful to tape her without Chloe's consent, I need proof if I complain to the education department. I could use my phone, but it would give the game away if it rang. Let me ask the electrical store if they have a recorder to do the job."

A late run into town provided Jacqui with the necessary equipment. It was a small, voice-activated tape used by secretaries for dictation. There were eight hours of recording time and five distinct lines for taping over the course of one day. As it was no bigger than a mobile phone, it was easy to conceal. She and Sid spent time reading the instructions and practising recording, so Jacqui was all set for the next day. Jacqui decided that replaying the tapes at the weekend was better than listening to them each night. She tried to verify Christopher's accusation that Chloe had posted a lookout, and even though Jacqui walked into Chloe's classroom over the next five days, she never saw the guard.

Jacqui was slack-jawed as she and Sid listened to the tape. Jacqui's fists clenched, and she sat hunched forward, concentrating on the tirade spewing from the tape. There were threats and insults aimed at the children. They heard sobbing, which caused ridicule, disdain, and anger aimed at the weeping child. With a scowl that darkened his face, Sid sat, muttering under his breath.

The recorder proved that the lookout was in place and alerted Chloe to Jacqui's imminent arrival. The tone on the tape changed, and Chloe was speaking in a sweet way that shocked her pupils.

"Do I need to listen to all of this?" Jacqui asked.

"No, it will be more of this. What are you going to do now?"

"Contact the district office to alert them to the problem. I will take a day off to visit their office. I need to warn the parents so the kids can all develop sick tummies for a day.

"What day do you want to go?"

"I'll contact the district office and find out when it suits."

# Chapter Twenty-Nine

Sid and Jacqui drove towards Toolavale. The provincial centre had developed since Jacqui had been away, and new housing estates were everywhere. Traffic in the business sector was steady, and off-street parking was still available at this early hour. As they walked toward the district office, they chatted among themselves. Jacqui had warned the school's parents that she would be absent, and most of the kids had come down with a mysterious virus. A few unlucky souls had to go to school because their parents worked in Lonsdale and couldn't keep them at home.

When they entered the office, a secretary glanced up at them.

"Can I help you?" she inquired.

"Yes, we are here to meet with the director; he expects us. I'm Jacqui Stuart, and this is my friend Sid Newland."

"Take a seat; he won't be a minute."

When they entered the director's office a few moments later, Jacqui hoped the man didn't hold a grudge. Even though he had not helped restore the school, she hoped he would not be ineffectual this time. After shaking hands with them both, he got straight to business.

"We've spoken before, Miss Stuart. I hope that your request today is easier to handle."

"Yes, I believe so. There is a tape you need to hear. You need only to listen to the beginning; the rest is much the same," Jacqui said as she pulled the recorder out of her bag. She set the small device on the desk and clicked the on switch. The director's eyebrows raised when Chloe shouted and swore at the children. He jumped up from his chair and said,

"I hope you are joking, Miss Stuart."

"Sir, the recording is not a joke. This behaviour is what the lower school at Manwarring has to endure daily. Let me fast forward just a little."

The director listened as Chloe's sickly, sweet voice filtered through the room. Jacqui shut off the tape.

"I wasn't able to catch her shouting and swearing. I visited the room often, but I realised something was wrong, and she spoke pleasantly to the kids. One mother came and made a complaint. A lookout is stationed at the door. The child needs to tell her when someone is coming, and she reverts to semi-normal speech."

"This is shocking. How much of that have you got?"

"The machine has space for five days, so I did the five days. Sid and I couldn't tolerate listening to five days' worth of it. It might be better or worse; I'm not sure."

"Well, this will be easier than your last request, but it will leave you alone in a two-teacher school."

"If I can hire a teacher aide, we will manage fine," Jacqui said.

"I'll end her contract at the end of the term, but what do I do with her then?" said the administrator.

After the meeting, Sid steered Jacqui to a small café. They had started early that morning, and as Sid had another appointment that day, he decided they needed morning tea. Once the servers served the cups of tea and scones, he said,

"I have a confession. I have taken over from your mother in the bossy stakes. You have an appointment this morning to visit with Toni. Her monthly clinic was yesterday. I rang to say you might need to chat with her, so she postponed her departure. We have about half an hour before you need to go. Jac, I have watched you lose weight for ten or eleven weeks, and I'm concerned. You eat little, don't laugh, and the smile doesn't reach your eyes. People who don't know you think this is normal behaviour. I'm worried about you, and I hoped it might help to talk to another woman."

Jacqui looked at the concern on his face, and she felt a sense of shame. Sid had given her a home and had supported her emotionally, and all she had given him was worry. "Okay, mum, I'll go," Jacqui said.

He grinned at her in relief and then tucked into his scones and tea.

While Jacqui was with Toni, Sid's other appointment waited at a table in the Palladium Hotel. Jacqui's father nodded at the server with the drinks menu as the men shook hands. When they had ordered their drinks, Colin said,

"So, Sid, you tell me you have a business proposition that might help my daughter. I wasn't aware that she needed help. Every time Margaret rings her, she says things are fine."

Sid nodded. "Sure, that's what she tells you, but I live with her and can say she isn't fine. I got her to meet Toni, the psychologist she talked to after the attack. That's where she is now. If you saw her, it would dismay you at how much weight she has lost and her overwhelming sadness. Jacqui puts on a wonderful display for people who don't know her well. But the smile never shows in her eyes, and she doesn't laugh much anymore. Her teaching isn't taking her mind off her problem, only exacerbating it, as she must teach with Brett's latest border. That's where I thought you might help me with my idea. If we can work out a basic arrangement, we can run it past her to see if she agrees."

"Okay, tell me about your plan."

Jacqui left Toni's office with a spring in her step and a plan of action circling through her brain. Talking to Toni was the tonic that Sid thought it might be. Jacqui scanned the street looking for him, but couldn't see him anywhere. A glance at her wristwatch told her she was early. A bench in front of a shop further along the street sounded like the ideal place to wait. As she strolled towards the seat, she saw Sid hurrying along the path towards her. He glanced up and noticed her, a smile flitting across his face as he gave her the once-over.

"Looking good, kid," he said.

"Thanks, Sid. I feel much better after talking to Toni. She gave me some perspective and a plan of attack."

"Well, my business went well, and as it involves you, we need to talk about it, but I prefer we sort it out at home," Sid said.

# Chapter Thirty

With the school term ending, the Department notified Chloe that they wouldn't renew her contract in the New Year. Her attitude towards Jacqui became poisonous, and Jacqui awaited her departure with anticipation.

While Sid's project raised Jacqui's spirits, a constant shadow hung over her. The fear of running into Brett in the street plagued her. Sid could shelter her locally, but couldn't protect her from the upcoming trial. He noticed her reluctance to venture into the small business district and tried to take the pressure off by doing most of the fetching and carrying himself.

With the court case date set, Jacqui needed to be in court each day. The prosecutor who took her statement said it should be a quick affair because the police caught the attacker in the act. The length of the trial didn't concern Jacqui. Recalling the attack worried her for the jury. The recitation would reignite her anger and self-loathing, which had dimmed over the intervening months.

She was nervous about meeting Brett and watching his face harden when he saw her, and the disgust in his eyes would undo her. She decided his defection stemmed from his inability to forget her violation. She could block out the attack while working with the kids, but she never stayed late at school. To her, it was asking for trouble. Sometimes, a stranger's voice raised in anger would make the fear return. The knowledge that the assailant was in custody didn't stop the dread from kicking in.

Jacqui and Sid waited on the steps of the courthouse. Colin was to meet them there, and Jacqui scanned the traffic, looking for her father's car. A hand on the shoulder made her whirl around, her eyes wide, and a gasp escaped her lips. Her Dad stood behind her, his face showing his distress when he realised he had frightened her.

"God, I'm sorry, Jac. I didn't mean to scare you."

"It's okay; I'm nervous." With her stomach doing somersaults and her fingers trembling, she conceded she was more than a little jumpy, more like scared stiff.

"Let's go inside before I have to meet anyone else," Jacqui said.

Sid's gaze met Colin's, and they both knew the thought of running into Brett frightened her.

They entered the courtroom. It was as Jacqui expected. The seats faced forward, and the judge sat at a desk in front of them. A single chair, located to the left of the bureau, seated the witnesses.

When the prosecutor came in, he acknowledged Jacqui with an inclination of his head and then patted the seat next to him. She reluctantly left her father and Sid and took a seat in the front row.

"God knows why we're here," he said. "How can he plead not guilty when two people caught him in the act? I'll try to make the judge rule on the evidence straight away," said Chris, the prosecutor.

As Jacqui sat waiting for the court proceedings to start, the guards walked in with a man. His hair was neat, and he appeared cleanly shaven; he wore a suit and tie. He smiled at Jacqui, and her skin crawled. Her breathing came in gasps, and her throat closed over.

"I can't do this," she said to Chris. He patted her arm and said, "You have to. Do you want him to attack another girl? If you don't testify, he may walk."

The trial began, and Chris approached the judge's counter to convince the judge to rule on the evidence without a hearing. She declined his request, stating that the trial must proceed because the defendant pleaded not guilty. Chris produced the police officer who made the arrest, and Brett was an eyewitness. With Brett on the stand, Jacqui kept her head bent, not wanting to make eye contact with him. Both witnesses told what they saw, and the defence attorney questioned them. Did they misinterpret what they saw? Could this have been consensual but just got out of hand? Brett's replies were scathing, and the judge directed him to answer yes or no.

Jacqui realised that the defence attorney intended to discredit her, thereby leading the jury to question the authenticity of the evidence. He asked Brett about his relationship with Jacqui. When Brett answered that they were friends and he had been her landlord, the opposing attorney sneered at him. She had gone out with a contractor who worked at the school. Did he hear the reports of that date spoken of in the pub? Now she lived with an older man; did Brett believe he was both her friend and landlord? As the attorney continued to badger him, his answers grew shorter, and his temper began to flare. The prosecutor objected, stating that the attorney wasn't questioning Brett but was harassing him. With the judge concurring, Brett's time in the witness chair was finished.

The public prosecutor called the ambulance officers, the on-duty doctor, and the nurse during Jacqui's hospital admission. The defence attorney could do nothing because these witnesses dealt with the facts that the hospital staff collected that night. When the doctors admitted Jacqui to the hospital, a nurse took photos of Jacqui's injuries, and she provided them to the investigation officer and logged them as evidence. As the jury viewed the pictures, Jacqui knew they were looking at them and then at her, trying to connect the dots. She saw one woman shake her head, and another put her hand to her mouth to stop a gasp from escaping.

With a sigh of relief, Jacqui smiled at the prosecutor. He had demonstrated that this attack occurred and that the sober, clean-cut man sitting next to his solicitor was the perpetrator. She was sure it was over. The defence attorney spoke to the judge, who announced a brief break before the defence presented its case. As they left the room, Jacqui glanced up, and her gaze collided with Brett's. She inhaled; her pulse sped up, and her stomach lurched. All rational thought fled from her brain as she looked into Brett's eyes. Her father grasped her arm and walked her through the door to the waiting room. A wave of dizziness hit her as she sank into the nearest chair.

When they returned to the courtroom, the defence attorney called his client to the stand. With well-aimed questions, the man shredded Jacqui's reputation. They depicted her as an opportunist, taking advantage of Brett and flaunting her relationships around the town. He repeated Peter's version of their date, which the prosecutor objected to because it was hearsay. When her attacker stated that Jacqui had invited her to meet him at the school and that the sex was consensual, she jumped to her feet and shouted, "You're a liar! You know it's not true."

"Sit back in your seat, Miss Stuart, or I'll have you removed," said the judge.

"But he's lying."

"Miss Stuart, I won't warn you again. Sit and be quiet, or I'll have you removed," the judge said.

Jacqui slid into her seat, her face tight with anger. She wrapped her arms around herself and rocked back and forth. Chris tapped her on the forearm. "I'm sorry, but I will have to put you on the stand. Despite your injuries, some jury members wonder if your account is true. We need to nail this jerk. Are you game?" he asked her.

Jacqui sat on the solitary chair and answered Chris's questions. No, she did not ask this man to meet her; the sex was not consensual, and she received injuries when he punched, slapped, bit, and raped her. She was weeping by the time Chris finished.

As she stood, preparing to return to her chair, the defence attorney said, "Miss Stuart, I have questions."

Jacqui nodded and sat down. He asked, "Had you met my client before?" and "Why did you go to the school that night?" His questions made the jury doubt her honesty and whether the assault was her fault.

When the opposition solicitor rested their case, Chris asked to call a late witness as the defence repeated a story the accused relied on to discredit Jacqui. The judge decided to review the evidence in her chambers, and if it were relevant to the case, she would allow it in court.

Peter looked sheepish as he sat in front of the judge. Chris asked him to retell the evening he and Jacqui had dinner in Lonsdale. The judge reminded him that he would be under oath if he took the stand, so what he said now needed to be a truthful account of the evening. Peter recounted the events of the night. When he finished, Chris said, "So why was the accused so sure Jacqui spent the night with you? Why did you tell everyone that she would sleep with anyone for the cost of a meal?"

Peter groaned and ran his hand across the back of his neck. "Everyone knew we met for dinner because I told them. I made stupid comments beforehand about my prowess. I needed to save face somehow. It never occurred to me that anyone would accost her. I'm sorry, Jacqui," he said.

When the jury returned, a 'Guilty' verdict was so welcome that Jacqui couldn't hold back a sob. It was over. Now, she could get on with her life.

# Chapter Thirty-One

With the case out of the way, Jacqui concentrated on Sid's new project. At first, his decision to buy the now-defunct pub in Manwarring stunned her. His logic that the townsfolk needed a meeting place was sound, and he intended to make it a more family-friendly atmosphere than before. Together, they tossed around various ideas. Eventually, they decided bed-and-breakfast accommodation was more practical than full accommodation with meals. Sid assured her that he had a private backer, and his builder's licence was still valid, even though he had not done any major construction for a long time.

"It's like riding a bike; you never forget how."

"It's a long way to drive backwards and forwards from your place," Jacqui said.

"Why don't we clean the residence and move in there?"

"Okay, that's a good idea. I won't have to travel so far to work. What will you do with your place?"

"A bloke has been bugging me to sell my property. I'll see if he wants to rent, and if he does, it will give me time to decide whether to sell."

With the residence refurbished and the dog fences secured, the two friends settled into their new accommodation. Sid spread the plans for the rest of the pub onto the large kitchen table.

"Jac, come and check the plans and tell me what you think."

As she sat, the backyard erupted from the sounds of a dogfight. The vicious sounds made the dogs run for the back door, as the dogs never fought. Sid barged through the door and shouted for the dogs to heel. Barney obeyed immediately, but Molly was reluctant to follow the command until Sid repeated it. After instructing the dogs to lie, he walked around the yard to see why they were fighting.

"God, look at that." He pointed to a mass of something on the ground.

"It's meat?" she said. Sid nodded, his face ashen at the thought of the outcome of this latest incident.

"I'll bet it's baited meat. I never taught Molly to eat only on command, so Barney must have been trying to stop her from eating the meat. Can you get me a bag, and I'll pick up the pieces? We have to take them to Trent, but we must check the yard each time the dogs go outside. I'll take the time to teach Molly only to eat when given the command. We'll use a password that only you and I know; that should keep them safe."

Jacqui stared in disbelief. "How can this still be happening? Someone trashed my car while I was away, and it continued as soon as we moved into town. Someone hates me."

"This is absurd and becoming more dangerous. It's time to hassle Trent into doing more investigating."

With Sid diverted by the need to teach Molly a new rule, Jacqui busied herself with tasks that needed to be completed before they could move on to the hotel's interior.

The hotel had deteriorated into disrepair. During its closure, no one had maintained the hotel, and the premises were in disrepair. Sid stripped the main rooms and started again. The bar was the only item he left in the public space, and he then refurbished it in a family-friendly manner. Tables and chairs sat atop gleaming, polished floorboards, and by stripping the bar and resurfacing it, the room took on a warm, welcoming ambience.

During their busy days, Sid watched Jacqui and knew his suggestion to her father had been a good one. Working on something new held Jacqui's interest, and while enjoying herself, her smile came more often. The shadow cast by the break with Brett rarely intruded on their work during the day. At night, he hoped she was tired enough to sleep without regrets.

Sid kept in regular contact with Colin, and his close association enabled him to understand the man better. He wasn't a weak man, but he decided long ago which battles to fight. Jacqui was one of the few individuals her father didn't intend to lose, so helping as a silent partner was vital to him.

The renovation was moving along well when Sid yelled out.

"Hey Jac, see what I've found!"

She put her paintbrush on the tray and walked to the kitchen, where Sid stood, peering at a hole in the floor.

"Ye gods," she said. "This room has floorboards!"

"Don't be a smart alec," he said. "There is a cellar under there. The pipes lead up to the bar. The publican of the day stored the kegs here, and the taps upstairs were connected to them. I might check it later."

"Great, just as long as I don't have to paint it."

Sid put his arm around her and kissed her on the cheek. "Your painting days are almost finished. Never again will I ask you to pick up a paintbrush."

She laughed as she walked back towards her painting job.

Sid and Jacqui sat in the beer garden, sharing a well-earned break, while the dogs lolled on the ground at their feet, occasionally looking up in the hope of a titbit. As she looked around, Jacqui thought about the challenge ahead of her to restore the garden to its former glory. She needed to call on local nurseries and experienced neighbouring gardeners to make this a shady retreat. The mood of the pub had changed. Now, the lovely old building looked welcoming. Her memory of the hotel as she had first seen it didn't compare with what she and Sid had done.

As she contemplated the garden renovation, Jacqui caught a whiff of smoke. As she jumped to her feet, she heard Sid say

"What the hell?"

They hurried to the side of the pub, and the sight of flames shooting out of the skip bins they installed for the renovations shocked them. The fire licked the edge of the wall, threatening the entire building.

"I'll call the fire brigade!" Jacqui yelled as Sid rolled out the hose stored on the fence line.

Jacqui raced inside and, after her call, came back to help.

The fire brigade arrived just as Sid brought the first bin under control. They doused the second bin and hosed the wall of the pub. Trent came minutes later and pursed his lips.

"I think I need to help with this. It's getting dangerous, but no one has seen any unusual happenings. Maybe forensics from Lonsdale might shed light on these attacks."

Brett was in town often enough to have heard the reports of the attempted baiting of the dogs and the fire in the skip bins. While the attacks seemed directed at Jacqui, he thought they were aimed at him. He wanted to offer his support to Jacqui and Sid, but was worried about how he would be received.

Sitting at his table, he wondered how it had all gone wrong. When Jacqui returned to Kyogle, he knew her mother would use her influence to have her stay there. The e-mail that shattered his world had come unexpectedly, and he still wondered how she could have ditched him so fast.

It had been hard to trust her and let her into his life. He needed to stick with his mantra, 'If it seems too good...' He should have held fast to his beliefs and moved her before giving her his heart.

He agonised over all that had gone wrong, but it did nothing to appease the hurt. Without Jacqui, the dogs and Sid's friendship, Brett decided to sell the farm and move. Could he forget her if he moved to another town and worked at something other than farming? Ironically, the decision his aunt had tried to force on him was now his chosen outcome. Once he paid his debts, he could start again somewhere else; he had to decide where. The further away from here, the better, he thought.

The one thought that kept circling in his mind was Where is Mr Right? There had been no other man in town visiting Jacqui. Wouldn't a new boyfriend contact her during the weeks she had been away from Kyogle? Brett had seen her fleetingly in town after the trial, and she was always with Sid. Where the hell was the new boyfriend? Could the relationship have ended? Jacqui's email asked him not to contact her; would it be wrong to ignore that request? He could use checking on her welfare as his excuse, but would she talk to him or hang up the phone? Surely, if her mother-approved beau were no longer in the picture, she would call him if she wanted to rekindle their relationship. Unsure of what to do about his dilemma, he opted to do nothing.

# Chapter Thirty-Two

After a long soak in the bath, Jacqui said goodnight and headed for her bedroom. A loud noise jolted Jacqui from sleep. Disoriented, her eyes bleary from sleep, she listened for any more sounds. She lay down again, but a cracking sound jolted her upright. Grabbing her robe, she slipped her thongs on and raced into the hallway. She collided with Sid as he attempted to reach her room. "Get out!" he shouted. "The back rooms are on fire. Go, go, go!"

As she ran to the front door, he yelled, "I've got to get the dogs. Call the fire brigade. I'll be right behind you."

The smoke choked Jacqui as she raced for the front door. It was hard going, as the electricity had gone out and the pub was pitch black inside. The pub's layout was simple to navigate in daylight, but now she moved by memory. When she reached the front door, she cursed as she fumbled for the handle. The locks were engaged, and she wasted time sliding the bolts and catches. After wrenching the door open, she staggered out into the street. Coughing from the smoke, she doubled over. The neighbours had garden hoses trained on the blaze.

"It's fine, love," said the man from across the street.

"We've called the fire brigade."

"Sid is still in the pub. He went to get the dogs. I have to go back," screamed Jacqui.

The neighbour grabbed her, "You can't go inside. If he's still there, we can do nothing for him now."

Wracked by coughs, Jacqui started when blood-curdling screams pierced the air. She whirled around. And before her was the most horrific thing she had ever seen. A person ran from the building's side door, engulfed in flames. Clothes and hair alight, the person ran away from the burning building. The nearest bystander grabbed the creature and threw it to the ground, rolling it over and over to quell the flames. Garden hoses, previously trained on the burning building, now pointed at the smouldering body.

Finally, the firefighters arrived. One firefighter kept the burned body wet while the others battled the flames in the building. Amid coughing fits, Jacqui approached the crumpled form on the ground. Disgusted at herself for her relief, she turned to stare at the burning building. Although it was hard to make out the person's appearance, their physique was too slight to be Sid's. Jacqui moved away from the damaged body and grabbed a firefighter.

She grabbed a firefighter."You have to find Sid. He's still in there," she said.

The firefighter shook his head. "Sorry, love, if he's still in there, we can do nothing to help him."

Jacqui collapsed to the ground. She rocked backward and forward with her knees tucked up to her chest. The firefighters, police, and locals all moved around her. A sad, keening sound escaped her, and the tears poured down her face. Suddenly, a hug engulfed her. Warm, powerful arms held her, and she knew instantly who it was. He lifted her to her feet, turned her to face him, and brushed the hair from her eyes.

"I'm sorry, Jac. He was a good man. God, I'm sorry," Brett said.

Jacqui huddled into his body, and the sobs continued. He rubbed his hand across her back; the action was meant to comfort. What did you say to someone who lost their mentor and great friend? No platitudes could lessen her grief, and while time was supposed to heal, he couldn't imagine a time when this wouldn't hurt her. Brett's refusal to speak to Sid would haunt him forever. It wasn't Sid's fault she had split with him, yet he had taken it out on his only good friend.

Once the fire brigade had the blaze under control, the police officer on the scene attempted to interview Jacqui. Her eyes were unfocused, and although the sobs had stopped, the tears flowed freely down her cheeks. She looked at the constable, her eyes glazed and her face blank. When he repeated his questions, Brett interrupted.

"For god's sake, man, stop! Can't you see she's in shock? She's in no fit state to answer questions. See her tomorrow; a few hours will change nothing."

The ambulance had departed the scene some time ago with its grizzly patient on board. When it returned, the paramedics wrapped Jacqui in a blanket and strapped her to the stretcher. She held on to Brett's hand and refused to let go, even when the ambulance officer needed to check her.

She wanted to forget and rid her mind of the pictures of the burning building. She tried to block her ears so she couldn't hear the flames' roar or the burning person's screams. Her eyes closed tight; she didn't see the silent exchange between the ambo and Brett. She felt the slight sting on her arm and then blessed oblivion.

When she woke, Jacqui lay still, trying to remember where she was and what had happened. The light filtered in through the windows and the ajar door. Looking at the white, unadorned walls, the memory of the fire returned to her in a rush. A wave of grief swept over her. She moaned, and Brett materialised by her side.

"It's okay, Jac. I'm here. It will be all right. Your parents are on their way."

He collected tissues and dabbed at the tears streaming down her face.

"Sid was such a good friend," she sobbed. "I loved him; now he's gone, and so are the dogs. I can't bear it. It hurts so much."

Brett hugged her tight and said, "We'll work it all out. Don't let your mother pack you up and take you away again. When you feel better, we need to talk."

A noise in the hallway and a strident voice making demands made Brett jump up. Not wanting to face Jacqui's mother made him look cowardly, but he was sure his presence would only incite her. He could stay where the conversation was audible, and if Jacqui needed help, he could be in the room instantly.

"I will move into the adjoining room; your mum will flip if she sees me here. If you need me, yell out, and I'll come and rescue you," Brett said. He kissed her on the cheek and left quickly.

Her parents entered the room, and Jacqui braced for her mother's caustic comments, but her father spoke first, and it shocked her to see how distressed he looked. His eyes were red, and his face was wreathed in sorrow.

"Jac, I'm sorry. Sid was a good man, and he loved you. You will miss him forever, but imagine if you had never met him."

"I can't believe he's gone. How do I manage without him? He has played a big part in my life. I'm not sure how to start again."

Colin looked at his daughter. She was as sad as he had ever seen her. Large black circles under her eyes added to the sadness. The only way to start the healing process was to have her released from the hospital. After that, he had no idea. Jacqui's decision to move back in with her mother was not a choice; it was a necessity. The two women in his life had always had issues. After Margaret's interference during the last visit, Colin was sure that Jacqui would resist any attempts to get her to return home.

He cast his mind back to the meetings and phone calls with Sid. His love for Jacqui had been genuine, and his suggestion had begun her healing. Where did he go now? God, he, too, would miss the old-timer.

"I might see what the doctors say and when they will release you. Back in a tick," said Colin.

When her father walked out of the room, her mother spoke.

"Jacqui, you have made emotional connections to two men; God only knows why. You have a family, and it's time you returned home to fulfil your responsibilities."

Jacqui peered through her swollen eyes and said, "What might my responsibilities be?"

"I had two children, but with your brother overseas, you have to return home, find a husband, and become a wife and mother. This teaching stuff is only a fill-in, not a career, and it's time you admitted that."

Jacqui let out a harsh laugh. "I guess you have a husband in mind?

"Yes, in fact, I do. Simon Branson comes from an excellent family; he has a prestigious job as a lawyer and was fond of you at one stage. I'm sure he'd jump at the chance to become reacquainted with you."

"What happens if I don't want a prominent lawyer as a husband? The guy was a pompous ass and an insufferable know-all."

"Jacqui, it's time to grow up. I got rid of the hick farmer for you, and now nature has done away with the old codger. You need to stop playing and come home."

"What do you mean you got rid of the hick farmer?" Jacqui hissed.

"Don't be naïve. You left the computer open; your code isn't that complicated. I sent an email to Brett saying you were ending your relationship. You should thank me; he'll grow into a dead bore, and you'd have to work as a labourer on the farm."

Colin walked back into the room and looked from one to the other. He could tell from their expressions that they were arguing. Jacqui sat up in bed and jeered at him.

"Did you know she sent an e-mail to Brett from me ending our relationship?"

Colin looked from one to the other and said, "You've got to be kidding!"

Margaret glared at her husband. "What did you expect me to do? You did nothing to stop her from becoming a labourer on that washed-up farmer's property. She must find a professional man with excellent prospects, not a no-hoper."

"Get out!" Jacqui screamed. She reared up on the bed, and with clenched fists, she glared at her mother. "Get the hell out of my life. I never want to see you again. You're an evil, cunning woman, and I hate you!"

Margaret looked at her husband for support. Colin held up his hands, backed up, and looked at his wife.

"When we married, I knew you were manipulative and a social climber, but I thought I could overlook those traits. When your aspirations for social betterment hurt my daughter, you've gone too far. I agree. Best you leave now because I don't want you here either."

As Margaret turned to leave, Brett barrelled into the room.

"Jac, get out of bed. I have a surprise for you."

He moved over to the bed and all but pulled her out. Her father moved forward to stop him, but Brett's glare levelled at him and stopped him in his tracks. Jacqui's feet hit the floor, and Brett supported her as she stumbled forward.

"For God's sake, can't you see she's in no fit state to run all over the hospital?" Margaret, held in place by Brett's arrival, snapped the question at him. He ignored the woman and gently lowered Jacqui to the floor. She sat on the ground, looking bemused. Her head tilted to one side, and she questioned Brett with her eyes. He rushed to the door and whistled. Two whirling bundles of fur dashed into the room. When they saw Jacqui, they both rushed to her. Barney was in her lap, and Molly ran backwards and forwards between her and Brett, yipping.

Jacqui was laughing and crying simultaneously. Sobs wracked her body as she clung to Barney and pulled Molly towards her. The younger dog was too excited to sit, and Brett had to restrain her with his voice commands as her exuberance threatened to topple Jacqui.

"Sid went back to get them. Where were they found?" Jacqui asked.

"They were in the cellar. It was the barking that alerted the clean-up teams. They couldn't enter the basement until Sid told them, "Say hello" ....

"They're friends", Jacqui finished for him.

Jacqui's hand flew to her chest, and her face showed comprehension. Her tired eyes opened wide, and she gave a loud gasp.

"Is he here? Is he all right?"

Brett beamed at her. "Yes, and yes," he said.

The door opened, and a nurse wheeled Sid into the room. Jacqui noticed he looked worn and old for the first time since she had known him.

"Crazy old man. He insisted on seeing you before we could treat him. Okay, now you have. We need to leave." With that, she whirled the chair around to exit the room.

"Stop!" Jacqui shouted. She rushed towards Sid.

"I want to hug you, but don't want to hurt you."

He held out his hand, and Jacqui gripped it. He pulled himself up, and she stepped in to steady him.

"Let no one say I knocked back a hug from a good sort," he joked.

She wrapped her arms around him, and he reciprocated. They stood, holding on to each other for a few minutes, and then the nurse thrust Sid back into the wheelchair and disappeared out the door with him.

# Chapter Thirty-Three

Seated at the kitchen table, a mug of tea held between her hands, Jacqui looked at Brett. The brown hair that was too long and the slight stubble on the face she knew so well calmed her battered heart. Even though she was reluctant to shatter the peace that enveloped the kitchen, the two needed to talk, and she needed answers.

"Brett, what happened?"

"I could ask the same thing. When you came to collect your things, you looked upset, but why were you distressed after the email you sent?"

"Ah, the email. Can you print the letter?"

Brett gave her a puzzled look, then walked out of the kitchen. The computer fired up, and a moment or two later, the printer's whirring sound filtered into the kitchen. When Brett returned to the kitchen, he handed the email to Jacqui without saying a word. Her fingers clenched, and her jaw hardened as she read the letter. Her mother had played on Brett's kind nature and integrity, imploring him not to contact Jacqui if he cared for her. She had ended the relationship and blocked communication between the couple.

Jacqui looked up and sighed.

"God, this letter is worse than I imagined. I didn't send this email. My mother said she did me a favour at the hospital by getting rid of the hick country farmer. When I shouted at her, she defended her actions, saying that my password was easy to crack and that she had done what she believed was best. According to her, nature had taken care of the older man, so now I could go home, marry a man she approved of, and have children. The woman is delusional and malicious. Sid and I left heaps of messages. I needed to talk to you, but we only ever got the answering machine. Even after we left all the messages, you never called back. One night, Chloe answered. She said you had finished with me and that I should stop ringing." Jacqui raised hurt eyes to look at Brett.

"Damn, I knew the bitch considered me her meal ticket. I only got the message that you and Sid were coming to collect your things. I didn't listen to the actual recording; Chloe relayed the messages to me. Were you coming to collect your belongings?"

"No, I thought I was coming home until she said you were kicking me out. Why didn't you want the dogs? It was a double punishment; you ousted all three of us simultaneously. How could you have considered putting Barney to sleep and selling Molly?"

Brett shot to his feet. "What?"

"Sid and I took the dogs because your border said you didn't want them and were getting rid of them."

"God, spare me from a cunning woman. Okay, let's sort this out. I didn't want to get rid of the dogs. It was much harder to do the farmwork without them. Chloe didn't like the dogs and constantly complained, but I had no intention of getting rid of them. Next, I'd have rung back in a shot if I received even one of your messages."

"What about when you went out for dinner or the movies? She subjected me to a report on your weekly social outings," Jacqui asked.

Brett grinned. "Jealous, were you?"

"Yes, damn it! My heart felt like someone had ripped strips of it. Every report hurt."

Brett moved across the room and gathered her into his arms. She buried her face in his chest, and the vibrations of his voice tingled against her skin. "What did you say?"

"That woman and I went nowhere together; no movies, no dinner, not even grocery shopping. When I offered her accommodation, I thought it was for a short time. When you didn't return, she appeared to think it was a green light to go for me. The woman is crazy. It was you I wanted."

Jacqui tilted her head back and gazed into his face.

"I wanted you, too. All the time, my mother hassled me and placed pressure on me. I wanted to come home, but she blocked me from doing so. Brett, are we good?" He brushed his lips across hers.

"Yes."

Jacqui sighed with contentment. With the dogs on the floor next to her, a special treat —she told Brett —all was right with her world. After Jacqui and Brett held the conversation they should have had months before, they decided to follow through with their fledgling romance regardless of her mother's opinion.

Margaret was staying at the postmistress's house, and Colin would drive to the farmhouse once she had settled in. When she heard a vehicle in the driveway, Jacqui knew her father had arrived. Both dogs raised their heads as the car neared. A car door slammed, and the dogs lay back down when Colin knocked on the door. His smile widened at the domestic scene in front of him. Jacqui, surrounded by the dogs, sat at the table with Brett.

"Now that looks like domesticity. You two seem right at home."

Jacqui rose and hugged Colin.

"Dad, I'm sorry. I didn't mean to hurt your marriage, but Mum did a terrible thing, and her only concern was her social standing in the community."

"We will sort out our problems, Jac. Hopefully, she will mend her ways because she doesn't like not knowing what's happening. The suggestion that she stay with the postmistress was inspired. Time alone might make her reconsider her aspirations."

Over dinner, Colin discussed the pub's plans. As he had spent a few stolen moments at the hospital with Sid, both men agreed to tell Jacqui who the silent investor was. The hotel site needed a thorough cleaning. The architects began the new plans after the doctors had released Sid from the hospital.

# Chapter Thirty-Four

Brett and Jacqui settled into living together as quickly as they had initially. The one problem that plagued Jacqui was the uncertainty about the vandalism and the attacks. Were they related to the fire, or were they separate incidents? The person who set the fire died due to their malicious act, but was someone still out there just waiting for them to settle before starting the harassment again? Trent arrived one evening with the information they needed to ease their minds.

Investigations into the cause of the fire suggest that it was intentionally set. The person who ran from the pub died, but the evidence shows that she used an accelerant to start the fire. Brett, the woman, was your Aunt Gloria. Her hideout was a shearers' shed that had been vacant for a decade or more. We discovered her car parked a kilometre away from the hotel. She must have carried the petrol in a can that overflowed onto her clothes. When she lit the building, her clothes ignited. There is evidence that her fixation was on you, Jacqui. Photos of you, taken here at the farm and outside the school, covered the walls."

Jacqui went ghostly white, and her fingers shook as she put the glass of water in front of her.

"All of this trouble is my fault?" Jacqui whispered.

"Not at all," Trent said. "Madness becomes so all-encompassing that it allows no room for logical thoughts. If she hadn't fixated on you, it would have been somebody else: your friend Sid, for example."

Brett took Jacqui's hand across the table. As he held her hand, he ran his thumb across the top of it and gently squeezed. "The responsibility for what happened is not yours, Jac."

"Do you want to hear the rest, or will I tell Brett and spare you the details?" Trent asked Jacqui.

Jacqui sighed. "Let's hear the rest."

Trent nodded and continued. "In the hut, we found your aunt's journal. She blamed you, Jacqui, for Brett not selling the farm. At first, she tried nuisance tactics, and then concentrated on things more likely to cause friction between the two of you. Why she went after Jacqui, who was no longer living at the farm, remains a mystery, but we think she was delusional and half-mad at that stage. We are satisfied that your aunt acted alone and have therefore closed the case.

When Trent left, Jacqui got up from the table and paced. With her arms folded around herself, she let the tears fall.

"God, Brett, I'm sorry. This fire, the injuries, everything was my fault. None of this would have happened if I hadn't moved in."

Brett walked around the table to where Jacqui stood.

"Do you remember what you said after the attack at the school? I said If only you told me that the fault was with the degenerate who attacked you and that it wasn't my fault. Well, right back at you, sweetie. The responsibility lies with my aunt and not with what you did."

Jacqui nodded her understanding. When he pulled her against him, she rested her head on his shoulder. With luck, she could leave her guilt behind and together, they could move forward.

"Will the settlement from the insurance company pay for Sid and me to go shopping, Dad? I have nothing except these clothes, and Sid has nothing either."

Brett laughed. "Just like a woman. She wants to go shopping as soon as we have avoided the crisis."

Jacqui pulled a face at him. "I've been considering something else. Sid leased out his house when we moved into the pub. He can't go home, and if he could, I'd worry about him being by himself."

"Even if we asked him to, there's no way he would move into the house, Jac," said Brett.

"You're right. Why not overhaul the station hand's house? I've noticed it before and thought, what a waste to leave it to fall apart. I know it's rough now, but I'm sure it will come up fine with some TLC."

Her father looked at her. "You're going to renovate again?"

"There's not much to paint this time," she laughed.

Colin and Sid arrived home later that day. Still shaken by his ordeal, Sid happily took a back seat to the action. They had completed the hotel plans, and with Colin making frequent hospital visits, they implemented the plan. The renovation of the station hand's house was underway. The house was small, with one bedroom, an eat-in kitchen, a lounge room and a bathroom, so the renovation was completed quickly. The tiny house sat behind the cattle yards, under a copse of trees planted many years ago to shade its small garden. It would mean that Sid had privacy but was close enough should he need help.

During this busy period, Jacqui and Brett spent hardly any time alone. It frustrated Jacqui that constant obstacles impeded their relationship, but she consoled herself that she was back where she belonged.

The summer rain had eased the stock-feeding routine. As a future backup, Brett put in more pasture for the cattle to graze, or if the rain continued, he could bale and store it. Working on the ground and planting meant that Brett and Jacqui spent even less time together. With the summer holidays coming to an end, she took matters into her own hands. She told Brett she had booked a table at a restaurant in Lonsdale for tea and, after that, a movie.

Dressed and ready to go, Jacqui fidgeted as Brett finished his last job of the day. Even if he were super-fast in the shower, they would still push it to be in Lonsdale at the appointed time. As he strolled into the house, she looked at the kitchen clock. "Come on! We will be late!"

He grinned at her.

"It's okay; there's been a change of plans."

Jacqui glared at him; her eyes narrowed in annoyance.

"You had better not be telling me we will spend the night on the couch watching the footy."

"Cool it, sweetie. I'm sure you will appreciate the changes I've made. But we will be late if I stand here talking to you."

Brett ambled away, whistling as he went.

Jacqui tried to find out what Brett planned on the drive into Lonsdale, but no cajoling worked; he was tight-lipped and refused to tell her. When Brett pulled into a parking lot set aside for the patrons of the Lonsdale Arms motel, Jacqui raised her eyebrows in question. He grinned and shrugged.

"One night is not enough; I told the guys we'd return in three days. Plenty of chances to spend quiet time alone, if you get my meaning?"

"You bought clothes for us both?"

He looked pleased with himself, and a smile of satisfaction crossed his face. "Sure did. We are staying for a few nights, so you'll need gear for two days and things for the nights. Girls always need bits and pieces, so I bought what I thought you might use."

Jacqui's face flushed, and her pulse picked up as she realised how much further Brett had taken her planned night off. After checking into the motel, Brett asked the receptionist to book a taxi. The taxi they caught deposited them in a small side street. Their destination was the family-owned Italian restaurant at the end of the lane. The small, intimate restaurant was a far better choice than the more prominent place she had booked, and she smiled and squeezed Brett's hand.

"Thank you for changing our plans. It's not only a woman's prerogative to change her mind," she joked.

Brett drew the eyes of over one woman. Dressed in his suit and tie, his dark hair shining in the glow of the candles and a slight shadow showing on his jaw, Jacqui had the urge to growl like a feral dog protecting a bone. The only thing that stopped her from staking her claim was that Brett noticed none of the admiring glances, and his sole focus was on her. While he was good company tonight, Brett pulled out all the stops to be charming. Jacqui smiled and laughed throughout the meal and was sorry when it came to an end.

Her pulse rocketed when Brett took her hand and rotated his thumb across her palm. She shivered at the intimate touch and squeezed his hand in response.

"Happy?" Brett asked.

"Thanks for doing this. Over the last few weeks, I've felt pressured, and not having private time with you has been annoying. I love Dad and am glad to have Sid with us, but boy, do we need private time?"

"Let's go to our motel; I have another surprise for you."

"More?" she enquired with a lift of her eyebrows. "I feel like it's my birthday or Christmas."

One surprise Jacqui immediately saw was a large bottle of champagne in an ice bucket.

"Jac, before you kick off your shoes and sip champagne, I have to tell you something." Brett drew Jacqui down on the couch and sat beside her.

"When you left to return to Kyogle with your parents, I feared your mother would stop you from returning. I missed you daily, but knowing you intended to return kept me going. When that email arrived, it gutted me. My life on the farm wasn't worth living, and I decided to sell it and move somewhere that wouldn't remind me of you. I couldn't imagine staying at the farm with memories of you haunting me. I lost you once, but I won't survive if you leave me again."

Jacqui gasped as he knelt on one knee.

"You are the love of my life. My life is worth nothing without you in it. Will you marry me?"

Jacqui looked at the man she had once loved and lost. She had no intention of losing him again and vowed to fight to keep him.

"Brett, my love, I have no intention of leaving you again. So, yes, I will marry you."

Brett found the small box he had put in his pocket before leaving the farm. He opened it for Jacqui and observed her face. Her eyes grew large, and her smile widened. The ring, exquisitely designed with small diamonds dotting the band, featured a solitaire at its centre.

"It was my mother's ring. She would have liked you and wanted me to give it to my future wife."

"Oh, my God. It's gorgeous."

Brett slipped the ring onto her finger and pulled her forward for a kiss. The kiss was soft and light, but Jacqui deepened it, desire spiralling through her. Brett pulled her close and took control of the kiss. He gently explored her mouth when he slid his tongue between her lips. The kiss became rougher and more possessive as she responded by flicking her tongue against his. Sliding his hands down her back, he pulled her tight against him. When she squirmed against him, he groaned and deepened the kiss, ravaging her with lips and tongue. She responded by sliding her hands into his dinner jacket. When she removed the coat, Brett pulled the dress off her shoulder and cupped her breast. He flicked his thumb over the nipple, which hardened, and he lowered his head to lick and suck the little nub.

"Bedroom," Jacqui gasped.

When she woke the following day, a warm body wrapped around her, and as she opened her eyes, she saw Brett was awake and watching her sleep. She rolled towards him and snuggled against his side. Her sigh was of pure pleasure.

"What do you want to do today?" Brett asked.

"Hm, I need breakfast first. If I lie here much longer, you will have to listen to my tummy grumble."

"Do you want to do anything special while we're here?" Brett inquired.

Jacqui gave a wicked grin. "I'll come up with something."

# Chapter Thirty-Five

L ife resumed its hectic pace; the nights spent with Brett were just a sweet memory. Colin went home with the promise of regular visits to check the hotel's progress. Sid moved into the stationhand's house and was busy building dog runs for his rescue dogs. With Brett's success with the dogs, the neighbours had shown interest in the project.

The school's enrolment numbers dropped as grade six and seven students moved to the high school. Only a few children remained at the school in Manwarring, and Jacqui knew the department might close the school and bus the remaining students to Lonsdale Primary School. Pushing the gloomy notion from her thoughts, she re-engaged the children, who were still in holiday mode.

The sheer terror of being alone in the building after school hours dissipated, and Jacqui often worked late. One afternoon, after the children left, she heard a vehicle pull up to the school. With nerves skittering, she watched as a dust-covered SUV pulled up near the gutter. The man emerged from the car and looked at the buildings before going to the classroom block. Jacqui stood and pulled an aerosol can of deodorant from her bag. She moved to meet the stranger with the can clutched in her hand. The man's attire suggested a desk job despite the SUV he arrived in.

Jacqui surveyed the newcomer with narrowed eyes. His close-cut brown hair showed signs of greying at the sides, but his trim physique and muscular build confirmed that this man kept in shape. He smiled as he climbed the stairs to the schoolroom and held out his hand for her.

"Hi, I'm Brian Fletcher from head office. Given your enrolments, I guess you've been expecting contact from us?"

Jacqui shook his hand and then gestured for him to enter her office.

"Well, I guess I don't need this," she said, showing him the can she held.

"Hm, I'm not sure what I tell you won't make you sweat. Maybe you should keep it on hand just in case," Brian said with a grin.

"The thought of sweating doesn't scare me, but I don't know where to buy mace. This can is here for protection. I figure it will slow someone down if I need."

Sympathy shone in his eyes as he looked at her.

"Sorry, I should have phoned. I had forgotten about the incident that occurred here a while ago. You've recovered from the attack and taken precautions. Which out here in this secluded spot is wise."

"Depending on what you tell me, I might feel obliged to use it."

After Jacqui made Brian a drink, they exchanged pleasantries while they drank. Eventually, she said, "Okay, give me the worst first and then let's work backwards."

The bad news is that unless enrolments increase by twenty-five per cent, the department has set its sights on closing the school. The government has invested a substantial amount in modernising the school for the twenty-first century, so it would be a waste to shut it down and walk away. We are considering alternative uses for the site, and with the hotel's reconstruction and the provision of decent accommodation, we might host seminars and public courses here. We are still undecided.

"Forgive me for being self-centred, but what happens to me?"

"We could always find you another country posting, or, depending on what we do with the site, you could move into the TAFE organisation. You could run courses for us and host other courses and seminars."

"I wasn't considering a career change, and I have ties to this town now, so I don't want to move away. How soon will the school be closed?"

"Since term one has just started, it would be less upsetting if we moved forward at the end of the first break. The kids can start at the Lonsdale Primary School at the start of term two."

"That's fair enough. Will the kids be able to receive help with settling into the larger school? These kids only began using computers for tuition in the National Curriculum, and they will be well behind students who have used technology since they began school."

"Sure. Are you interested in attending Lonsdale's school for a term or two to help with the transition? By then, we should know what direction we're taking with the site here. What do you think?" he asked.

"A temporary appointment sounds good. If I'm there, it will help the kids settle, giving me time to get used to being something other than a classroom teacher."

As she drove towards Lonsdale on the first day of the new term, Jacqui chuckled at the irony of the situation. Her wish to avoid driving on this road was why everything happened to her over the last year. While she recognised the traumas she suffered due to her move to the country and her involvement with Brett, Jacqui was still content with her choices. Her life now held unprecedented dimensions. Her relationship with her father blossomed, the only hitch being her mother's refusal to accept Jacqui's engagement to the 'dirt poor' farmer. She also had the love and support of Sid, who mentored her like a grandfather.

With the hotel nearing completion, Jacqui broached the subject of wedding dates with Brett.

"Brett, with the hotel refurbished, we could hold our wedding there, but I need a date. There will be lots to organise."

His response was, 'As soon as you are ready.' So, taking him at his word, Jacqui organised the date and started preparations. After considering this, she decided the best place to hold the wedding was the renovated beer garden. The transformation was remarkable: the dirt floors were paved, the struggling plants were removed, and a series of lush gardens surrounded the patio. The cheap plastic tables and chairs gave way to stylish outdoor furniture, and they removed the shades, replacing them with shade cloth. Jacqui reasoned that using the outdoor space her father had designed was critical. It was no longer a venue for the rough, beer-swilling louts who frequented the bar in years past. She hoped to encourage other patrons to view the hotel in a new light by holding her wedding at the newly built facility.

Her cousin Jess was her bridesmaid, and her brother travelled from overseas to attend his sister's wedding. Jacqui's relatives booked the accommodation, and visitors and guests filled the motel for the first time. With the men at the farm, Jacqui readied herself for her big day in the motel bedroom with her cousin.

The only sadness associated with the day was that her mother had not replied to Jacqui's invitation. Every girl needed her mother present on her wedding day, but there appeared to be no reconciliation between the two Stuart women.

Jacqui's face was filled with excitement, and she wore a flowing white dress, her bare shoulders revealing a hint of cleavage. As Colin watched his daughter's face, despite what had occurred here, Brett and Jacqui were right for each other from the moment they met. They took a while to get together, and his wife's intervention complicated things, but watching Jacqui's happiness today was worth the hardship they endured.

As he walked through the room, decked out for the reception, Brett shook his head in astonishment at the lavish decorations and table settings. The round tables covered in white tablecloths sported shiny cutlery and floral centrepieces. China place settings, arranged with place cards, indicated which table each guest should sit at.

Champagne glasses glittered in the fading sunlight, and strings of lights twinkled like thousands of tiny stars. Balloons and streamers added to the room's festive air, at odds with the occasion's solemnity. Brett's forthcoming pledge to Jacqui had come after a lifetime of waiting, and he was eager to get on with proceedings.

Brett and Sid walked through the reception room to the patio, where the wedding would occur. Surrounded by guests in their finery, Brett could focus on nothing except the direction from which Jacqui and Colin would come. A firm hand on his shoulder dragged his attention back to his best man.

"Nervous, mate?"

"A little, but I feel excited. I shouldn't say this, but the sooner I get a wedding ring on Jacqui's finger, the better. Her mother will have no say in her life, and she can't take her away from me. Does that sound too possessive?"

Sid laughed. "Yes, but it's understandable after everything you two have endured."

Brett watched as Jacqui walked along the carpet with her father. Her face was alight with happiness. She looked stunning in her simple gown, and he wondered at his luck in winning her as his wife.

They had been through so much that Brett could barely believe she was here, and soon, they would begin their life together. His life changed the night he took Jacqui in, and the roller coaster ride since then had been filled with laughter and heartache. The two women who objected to their relationship mattered not to Brett, but he knew her mother's refusal to accept their marriage hurt Jacqui. His one regret was that his mother hadn't lived long enough for her to meet Jacqui. He was sure that his mother would have loved her. Colin handed his daughter to Brett and said, "Be happy."

Brett knew the wedding Jacqui had organised was not what her mother wanted. Besides wanting a professional man for her daughter, Margaret also wanted tuxedos and a large wedding party comprising business associates and members of her social circle. Jacqui wanted a small wedding with her brother, cousins, and best friend in attendance.

He felt grateful that she had gone for a simple wedding, limiting the guests to those who meant a great deal to her. The ceremony was brief; it was held up for a minute while Sid, the best man, searched for the wedding ring.

When the married couple turned to greet the guests, Jacqui smiled at Brett. He bent to kiss her on the cheek, and as he turned, he saw Colin talking to a woman. The woman turned; it was Jacqui's mother. Brett nudged her and nodded to show that she should look at the back of the row of seats. He felt her stiffen, and then, as her mother caught her eye, she nodded and smiled, making Jacqui's day complete.

## STARTING OVER

Thank you for joining me in telling the story of Jacqui and Brett. I hope you enjoyed their story as much as I liked recounting it.

If you loved the book and have a moment to spare, I would appreciate a brief review on the page or site where you purchased the book. Reviews from readers like you make a massive difference in helping new readers find stories like Starting Over. Your help in spreading the word is much appreciated.

Thank you!

Robyn C Rye

robyncrye.author@gmail.com

# Also by Robyn C Rye

**Farnsworth Sisters**
Marrying a Rogue
Rescuing Hannah

**The Buckingham Sisters**
Lady Maggie's Challenge
Layla's Unwanted Husband

**The Evans Family**
Sometimes Love is not Enough
Still the One
Moving Forward

**Standalone**
One More Chance
Lady Jayne's Reputation
Third Time's the Charm
Can't Stop Loving You

The Marriage Scam
An Unlikely Match
Searching For You
The Unexpected Suitor
The Lady and the Duke
Starting Over
An Unforgettable Stranger
The Duke's Revenge
The Temporary Wife
Against The Odds
Betrayed
No Good Turn Goes Unpunished
Lady Eloise's Soldier
Lillian's Forbidden Beau
Remember Me
Always Second Best
When One Door Closes
Coming Home to You
Chasing Shadows
Fool Me Once
Deserting Lady Audrey
My Unlikely Saviour
Lies and Deception
A New Beginning
Julia's Second Chance
The Hidden Enemy
The Maiden's Redemption
Miss Elizabeth's Season

9 798224 538263